IT WASN'T LOVE

Jimmy stood up, his face set and hard.

"I swear I'm going to protect you now, Lois," he said.

"But I'm—still—Philip's wife."

"I shall never rest until you are mine, Lois."

She was silent. Here in this little, sun-lit living-room—so typically a bachelor's room—she could be happy and at peace. If only Life would let her be. But there was no peace now. The atmosphere was charged with terrors, difficulties, vibrant with men's passions. . . . So it seemed to Lois.

Suddenly Jimmy walked to the window.

"Now for a row, Lois,' he said under his breath. "This is your car, and Sanpell's in it. He's come for you!"

GW00801702

**Also by the same author,
and available in Coronet Books:**

Put Back the Clock
And All Because
To Love is to Live
The Cyprus Love Affair
Forbidden
House of the Seventh Cross
The Boundary Line
Laurence My Love
Gay Defeat
Do Not Go My Love
All For You
I Should Have Known
The Unlit Fire
Shatter the Sky
The Strong Heart
Stranger Than Fiction (autobiography)
Once is Enough
The Other Side of Love
This Spring of Love
We Two Together
The Story of Veronica
Wait for Tomorrow
Love and Desire and Hate
A Love Like Ours
Mad is the Heart
Sweet Casandra
To Love Again
Arrow in the Heart
A Promise is Forever
The Sweet Hour
Nightingale's Song
Fever of Love
Climb to the Stars
Slave Woman
Second Best
Lightning Strikes Twice
Loving and Giving
Moment of Love
Restless Heart
The Untrodden Snow
Betrayal (Previously Were I Thy Bride)

It Wasn't Love

Denise Robins

CORONET BOOKS
Hodder and Stoughton

Copyright 1930 Denise Robins

First published in Great Britain by Mills and Boon 1930

Coronet Edition 1976

*The characters and situations in this book are
entirely imaginary and bear no relation to any real
person or actual happening*

This book is sold subject to the condition that
it shall not, by way of trade or otherwise, be
lent, re-sold, hired out or otherwise circulated
without the publisher's prior consent in any
form of binding or cover other than that in
which this is published and without a similar
condition including this condition being
imposed on the subsequent purchaser.

Printed and bound in Great Britain for
Coronet Books, Hodder and Stoughton, London
by Hazell Watson & Viney Ltd, Aylesbury, Bucks

ISBN 0 340 20736 1

CHAPTER I

By the time the Blue Funnel boat *S.S. Artis* had reached Port Said, Lois Mannering realised quite definitely that she was in love with Philip Sanpell.

She had been warned by numerous friends, before she set foot on board, against "sea-voyage flirtations". They were notoriously dangerous affairs. One felt so romantic on board ship under a hot, tropic blaze of stars and moon, with a charming man who could make one feel the "only woman in the world".

Philip Sanpell had made Lois feel that.

One night, sitting beside her in a secluded corner of the deck, when the boat was just steaming into Port Said, and the air was hot and breathless, and the moonlight a thing of beauty and magic, he told Lois that he adored her and wanted her to be his wife.

"But it's—it's absurd," Lois answered weakly. "We've only known each other a—a few days."

"Long enough for me to know that I love you, Lois," was his reply. "Oh, my dear, my dear, don't you love me, too?"

She looked at him; leaned back in her deck chair, thrilling with excitement. In the white moonlight, Philip's face was remarkably handsome. He was the most handsome man she had ever seen. A skin, ivory pale, which never seemed to tan under tropic suns; dark narrow eyes deeply set under straight black brows; very smooth dark hair brushed straight off his forehead.

To most women Philip Sanpell was dangerously

good-looking and attractive. Very few saw behind that perfect mask; very few noticed the thin cruelty of the lips under the dark, close-clipped moustache; guessed at the hot temper smouldering under the veneer of laziness and good-humour.

To Lois, inexperienced, just emerging from the quiet shell of a secluded life in a London suburb, Philip Sanpell was wonderful and without flaw. Life just at the moment spelt Romance and sunlight, and why should she peer behind that light and see the lurking shadows?

When Philip said: "I love you, Lois," it melted her; made her all soft, tender, yielding womanhood. She said:

"Oh—do you mean it—can you mean it?"

"You know that I do," he said. "And you know that you love me too, Lois."

She looked at him, flushed; starry eyed.

"I—do like you, Philip."

"Like . . ." he echoed the word with a low laugh. "I want to hear something more than that from you, my Lois."

"But you—know so little about me. I'm a very dull sort of person. I have nothing to commend me."

"Haven't you?" Again Philip laughed and suddenly caught both her hands and kissed them each in turn. "Why, you're the loveliest thing I've ever seen, darling."

She leaned a little towards him.

"The voyage has been very thrilling and wonderful and you have been very, very nice to me. . . ."

"I could be nicer," he said. "And we're only just at Port Said—we've got the rest of the voyage together. Say you'll marry me—sweetheart!"

The last word, spoken in Philip's husky, attractive voice, completely melted Lois. The next moment she was in his arms. He tilted back her head a little and then slowly, ardently, kissed her.

That kiss was a revelation to Lois. It seemed to take from her her last shred of resisting power. She was madly in love with this man. She did not want to resist him. She would marry him . . . of course . . . to be his wife would be the most miraculous thing life could offer.

Her arms went round his neck.

"Oh, Philip, Philip . . . I'm so happy. . . ."

He touched her lips lightly . . . ever so lightly; kissed the soft waves of her blonde, silky hair. He was very tender with her now . . . very subtle . . . he knew just how to play on the cords of her emotions as an artist plays on the strings of a violin. While he caressed her, he whispered a hundred passionate promises — made a hundred passionate vows.

The sound of music floated out to them from the saloon. Dreamily Lois listened. The orchestra was playing "Less than the Dust". Plaintive and haunting the Indian Love Lyric drifted on the still, hot air. Lois felt a sudden catch in her throat, and she shivered. It was as though the music seemed to hold some half-veiled warning. She pushed Philip away from her.

"No, Philip, don't kiss me again—it's so hot."

"Not so hot as it will be in Kuala Lampor," he returned, conscious of her sudden doubt.

"Kuala Lampor?" she repeated. "But I'm going to my brother in Singapore."

The man's dark eyes narrowed.

"No, darling—you're going to marry me and live in Selangor—up Kuala Lampor (K.L., as we call it out there). My bungalow is twenty miles outside the town."

Her breath came quickly, the fear of a moment ago had vanished.

"Oh, Philip, I—I shall have to see Dick first. We—can't get married till I've seen him—asked him."

A long argument followed. Outwardly the man was patient, gentle with her. Inwardly he was flaming with impatience and growing rage because this little soft, innocent slip of a girl was so self-willed and stubborn. Philip Sanpell was not used to being thwarted. But he was trying hard not to let that furious temper of his blaze out. He knew that it would be fatal to let Lois see under the mask before he married her.

He wanted her almost to madness. There was something peculiarly appealing in her to Philip.

She had told him everything about herself. Till now she had lived in London with a widowed mother; she had done nothing in particular. But now the mother was dead and Lois was on her way out to Malaya to her brother, Dick, who was doing quite well on a rubber estate which he had bought in partnership with an old friend from Cambridge.

There was nothing in the world to prevent Lois from marrying Philip—except Dick. Philip Sanpell had not the least desire to wait until the boat touched Singapore before he married Lois. Everybody in Malaya knew the name of Sanpell and a good many men had suffered at his hands, and were not likely to forget it. Dick Mannering might have heard tales. . . .

But Lois said "No" to all his arguments. Her little display of convention, of propriety, maddened the man. In this moment, just because she had beaten

him, he would like to have hurt her, physically . . .
thrashed her into submission . . . and kissed away her
tears.

The ship touched Port Said, then steamed on towards Singapore. The weather seemed to Lois to grow
hotter and hotter, and she could only sit on deck in the
thinnest of cotton frocks and languidly pass the long,
golden hours with Philip at her side.

Philip had ceased to argue about a marriage on
board. He was clever enough to know that Lois would
shrink from him if he harassed her. So he laid himself
out to be most charming for the rest of the voyage,
and on Lois's engagement finger there now shone a
brilliant diamond set in platinum. Philip had bought
that ring on board. One can buy everything for any
occasion on a liner these days.

Lois was blindly happy. Many women on board
seemed to envy her sudden possession of the lithe,
handsome man who was the most devoted and atten-
tive lover. She often asked herself, humbly, what she
had done to deserve such happiness.

Once Philip asked her if she had ever thought of
marriage with any other man. She said:

"No-o—not exactly."

"You sound uncertain, darling," he smiled at her.
"Come along—confess—I won't eat you up. You're
so pretty, Lois, I can't believe I'm the first fellow to
kiss you."

"Well—in the way you kiss me, yes, you are," she
said, her cheeks hot and pink. "But there was one man
—quite young—I was awfully fond of him and he
seemed to be of me. We were never engaged . . . it was

only one summer when Dick came home from the 'Varsity . . . brought Jimmy with him. . . ."

Philip listened to the shy confession that followed, with eyes half-contemptuous, half amused. Such innocence . . . such a white purity! it was amazing and yet really very adorable, he thought. Just a simple story. Dick Mannering's best friend at Cambridge had spent a summer on the river with Dick and his sister; two years ago, before Dick went out East to try his luck. Jimmy had gone punting with Lois . . . Lois described him as a sun-browned, good-looking, cheery boy . . . and one night on the river under the stars they had kissed . . . and she had thought that love had come into her life.

But it hadn't really come, she told Philip. It had just been a "boy-and-girl" affair; she at nineteen, Jimmy at twenty-three. He had had no money; they could not possibly become engaged. He had vanished out of her life entirely after that one summer.

Lois spoke of it without regret. It all seemed so childish after she had learned to love Philip Sanpell. . . . Yet she thought rather wistfully of Dick's friend, Jimmy Morgan. He had been a dear, and that night on the river when his boyish lips had touched hers lightly and innocently, she had thought that perhaps later on, a deeper, more passionate love might follow. For months she had treasured the memory of Jimmy; put his photograph on her dressing-table; made a hero of him.

She would always think tenderly of Jimmy. And Dick had, in his letters, spoken of him sometimes. Jimmy was out in Malaya with Dick now; often sent her friendly messages; hinted that he hoped to see her when he came back on leave.

But that was all passed and gone. With a little sigh she looked at the perfect face of the man she had promised to marry and who had come like a meteor into her life . . . flashing . . . wonderful.

She gave him her hand impulsively.

"There's been nobody but you, ever in this way, darling," she said.

He was not the least jealous of her innocent past. He kissed the little hand—kissed each slim, tapering finger separately. He knew that he was the first. And he did not for an instant pause to ask himself if he were worthy to take such innocence, or feel remorseful at what he meant to do in sweeping Lois off her feet and marrying her.

He thought of the life he had led in Malaya before they had met. He began to talk to Lois of his bungalow, his rubber-estate in Kuala Lampor; careful not to tell her of any incidents which might frighten or make her suspicious of his real character.

"I've made a bit of money; my estate is doing well," he said. "You'll be comfortable with me, Lois: I've just been home on leave, you know, getting a breath of fresh air. You can't live in Malaya for any length of time without a break, home. But I've got a topping bungalow. We'll be so happy, baby darling."

Baby darling! A silly name, yet it thrilled her. She said:

"Of course we will, Philip. But I don't want your money—only your love."

"You've got that right enough. Kiss me, Lois."

They were standing side by side in a secluded corner of the deck. The sun had set and the starlit splendour of night had replaced the hot glory of the tropic day.

Lois moved to her lover's side and he put his arms about her, towering over her from his great height. His dark, brilliant eyes were so ardent that they made her catch her breath. For an absurd instant she felt inclined to run away . . . to escape from him . . . then she felt his lips on her mouth and she went limp in his arms, yielding, adoring him. Again from below came that haunting melody: "Less than the dust beneath they chariot wheel." But this time Lois took no notice.

After she had gone to her cabin to dress for dinner, Philip Sanpell remained awhile where she had left him, and smoked many cigarettes.

His face was marred by a very unpleasant expression. He was thinking of one or two ugly incidents in his past; of that saying that "old sins have long shadows". How was he going to prevent Lois from running into one or two women out in Malaya with whom he had played fast and loose? And supposing Mannering knew too much . . . persuaded Lois to break with him? Philip's hand clenched at his side as he visualised Lois coldly breaking her engagement. God! How angry she made him when she showed the prim, reserved side of her. But he was not going to be thwarted . . . robbed of her. He would take her, break her before she could slip out of his hands. . . .

Down in her cabin Lois was putting on a new pink georgette sleeveless dress with a big flower on the shoulder. She looked at her reflection in the mirror with glowing eyes.

"I want to look pretty—for him," she whispered to the radiant girl in the mirror. "I love him so; I think I am the luckiest girl in the world to be marrying Philip."

When the *S.S. Artis* reached Singapore it was in the early hours of the morning. But Lois was up . . . standing by the rails with Philip at her side, her eyes wide open with excitement and interest, her hand tight clasped in his.

"Singapore . . . Malay States at last . . . Oh, Philip, I am so thrilled," she said.

Sanpell smiled tolerantly. Singapore meant nothing to him. It was only too familiar and an uneasy feeling about Dick Mannering hung over him this morning. He still felt secretly angry with Lois because she had refused to marry him on board.

Once he looked down at the girl's sweet little flushed face and said :

"Baby heart of mine; supposing your—er—er—your brother refuses to let you marry me—what will you do?"

Lois hesitated. Then she laughed.

"Why should he? He'll be as proud of you as I am, Philip. But if he doesn't want an immediate marriage, I shall have to think, shan't I?"

Philip's dark eyes narrowed to slits, his fingers closed so tightly round her hand that she winced with pain.

"No," he said in a voice of concentrated passion. "You won't have to think. I shall think for you. You're going to marry me, to-day, Lois. . . . I swear you are . . . before we leave this boat."

She caught her breath and stared up at him. The passion in his eyes and his voice overwhelmed her. But almost at once he was soft, tender, supplicating again.

"Dearest—dearest of all—don't be cruel to me . . . don't keep me waiting any longer. When Dick comes on board . . . let him be witness to our marriage."

The witchery of him stole over her, rendering her helpless; like wax in his hands. His face was incredibly handsome and tender once more. What woman could have resisted him? She leaned her fair little head against his arm; her cheeks hot, her eyes like stars.

"Oh, Philip darling—all right—I'll marry you to-day—yes, I will—I promise."

"Ah!" said the man, very softly under his breath, and his lips touched her silky head. But the look in his eyes was not good to see.

There followed a very disappointing hour or two for Lois. Dick Mannering failed to come on board. In vain Lois searched the crowd of white-clad men on the docks . . . watched each one who came up the gangway to greet mother, wife or sweetheart. But Dick, her big, tall brother was not there.

"I don't understand where Dicky is. He must be coming, surely," she said uneasily. "He knows when the *Artis* was due to arrive. He cabled that he'd meet me."

Philip, secretly pleased that Dick had failed to come, now used every power of fascination that he possessed to persuade Lois to marry him without delay.

"Let's give him a surprise. He's late—but he'll come soon. Let's get married and surprise him, Lois," he urged. "Lois, you want to be my wife, don't you?"

"Y—yes," she bit her lip and faltered. "Of course I do—but I wanted Dick to be present and—"

"Dick may be delayed—may not be coming at all," interrupted Philip, holding both her hands and looking at her with beseeching eyes. "And I've got an important business date in Kuala Lampor which I must keep. I've got to catch the coasting boat at Port Swettenham to-day. Unless you come with me as my wife, Lois, I'll have to leave you alone. It will madden me, dearest—to be separated from you when I adore you so—to let you go up country to your brother's estate all alone. . . ."

He went on pleading, cajoling. Lois listened. Her eyes still searched the crowd on the docks in a worried, anxious fashion. Then she looked up at her lover. His eyes were compelling now. . .

"Prove that you love me—Lois—my darling—"

She was lost. She was struggling with tears of disappointment because Dick had not come and she dreaded being parted from Philip. She surrendered weakly.

"Very well, Philip darling—I will—I'll marry you now."

So Philip Sanpell got his way. They were made man and wife; using the diamond engagement ring as a wedding ring. The captain officiated in the saloon, long after the other passengers had gone. There were only a steward and stewardess for witnesses.

Lois went up on deck with Philip again, feeling like one in a strange, romantic dream. The hot sun poured down upon them. Before her dazzled eyes lay Singapore shimmering in a blaze of golden sunshine . . . the harbour like a curve of blue glass sparkling, dotted with small boats. She was in Malaya . . . and she was no longer Lois Mannering. She was Mrs. Philip Sanpell. It was incredible.

"Now, darling," said Philip, "if your brother fails to

turn up, you can come to K.L. with me quite respect-
ably—can't you, little one?"

She flushed under the ardour of his gaze.

"Oh, Philip—" she began. Then she broke off
abruptly and gave a cry: "Oh, there's Jimmy! Jimmy
... of all people in the world!"

Philip's charming, teasing expression disappeared.
His face grew wary and not very agreeable as he saw
a tall, loose-limbed man in a white drill suit and
therai, who came striding up the gangway and on
deck towards Lois. Jimmy, eh? That must be Morgan,
the young Cambridge fool who played about with
Lois.

Lois ran towards her brother's friend; genuine
pleasure in her eyes.

"Jimmy!" she exclaimed.

He saw her and strode to her side gripping both her
hands.

"Lois—my dear! how are you?"

"Ever so well, Jimmy, but where's Dick?"

Morgan did not answer Lois's question for a
moment. He stood looking at her very gravely, a
strange, hesitant look in his eyes. Lois thought how
much older he looked.

Jimmy was very tall—his eyes were on a level with
Philip's. But he was built on a bigger scale than Philip,
who had rather a slim figure. Jimmy was broad-
shouldered. He had a square face burned bronze by
the sun, and a mass of light-brown curly hair. His
eyes were still the eyes of the old Jimmy, Lois decided. Very blue and bright in his brown face. But the
mouth was a trifle stern now.

She was genuinely pleased to see him again. Her
passionate love for the man she had married this

16

morning could not alter the old friendship and affection for Jimmy.

Morgan glanced at Philip. He wondered who this much too handsome fellow was at Lois's side. Lois saw the look and her face flushed.

"Oh, Jimmy, by the way—let me introduce—my husband—Philip Sanpell," she said proudly, if a little shyly.

If a bombshell had exploded at Jimmy's feet he could not have been more amazed.

"Your husband?" he repeated.

"Yes. I—I expect you're surprised. Dick will be too. I—I met Philip on board, and we—we were married this morning."

Morgan stared at the man. Sanpell . . . Philip Sanpell . . . the name sank into his mind and then suddenly a terrible feeling of disaster stole over him. Sanpell . . . yes, he had heard that name in Malaya . . . who had not?

Many unsavoury tales flashed into Jimmy's memory. Lois was looking at him with innocent eyes, oblivious of his thoughts.

"Are you very surprised, Jimmy?"

"Yes," he stammered. "I—I am—"

Now Philip spoke.

"Won't you congratulate us, Morgan?"

He spoke in a drawling voice, but there was defiance in his eyes. He was defying Jimmy to refuse them his congratulations. He knew exactly what lay at the back of Jimmy's mind. Exactly what Jimmy was remembering. Well, damn it, what had it to do with Morgan? Philip thought savagely.

Jimmy struggled with himself.

"I—Yes, of course—but—it's so very unexpected,"

at length he blurted out. "You see—Dick asked me to meet Lois and look after her."

"I'll be able to relieve you of that responsibility," said Philip with a sneer.

Lois—still unconscious of any disaster—looked happily from Philip to her old friend.

"Where is Dick?" she asked again.

Morgan pulled himself together. He had come with bad news for Lois, and he had better get it over.

"Look here, Lois," he said. "I'm terribly sorry. I don't know how to tell you, but poor old Dick—"

He stopped. Lois stared at him. All the brightness vanished from her face. Her heart gave a twist of fear.

"Jimmy," she said. "Dick isn't—isn't ill?"

"Worse than that. I'm afraid, Lois."

She went white to the lips and held out a hand blindly to Philip, who caught it.

"Jimmy—!"

"Lois, it's no use beating about the bush," he said wretchedly. "Dick caught a chill a few days ago, up on the estate. He—died forty-eight hours ago. He'd had bad fever lately—he wasn't any too strong. Lois, I'd rather anything than have had to come and tell you this."

He stopped dead. The heart-broken look in Lois's eyes cut him to the quick. She had not even known that Dick was ill.

She was stunned with grief. Dick dead . . . dead and buried! She would never see him again. She hung on to Philip in that first shock of grief and pain . . . crying bitterly. Philip held and comforted her. He was charmingly sympathetic. But in his heart he was profoundly glad. Mannering's death would relieve him of any necessity to fight over Lois and would save a great deal of unpleasantness.

"Oh, Philip, poor Dick . . . Poor, dear Dick," she sobbed pitifully.

"I'm awfully sorry for you, darling, but you've got me," he consoled her. "Thank God we are married."

"Yes, thank God we are," she said covering her tear-wet face with her hands. "What would I have done without you?"

Jimmy Morgan stood by feeling more uncomfortable and wretched than he had ever felt in his life. He hated to see Lois cry. But still more did he hate to think that she was married to Sanpell. When Dick had died up there in their bungalow in the hills, Jimmy had taken a solemn oath to look after Lois for him. Dick's dying words had been:

"Take care of my little sister, Jimmy . . . she'll be alone in the world now. Promise you'll take care of her."

And Jimmy had said:

"You know I will. If I had a bit more money, I'd ask her to marry me. Perhaps one day I'll do it yet, Dick."

Yes, that was what he had meant to do. He had never forgotten the sweetness of Lois that summer on the river. He had been waiting for his financial position to improve. It was a bitter disappointment to have met Lois again only to find that she had married another man. If it had been any other man than Sanpell, Jimmy would have wished them luck, and tried to forget. But Philip Sanpell . . . this man who had such a hideous temper . . . such an evil reputation with women. . . . It would have broken Dick's heart to see his sister married to Sanpell.

"Don't worry about me, Jimmy," she said presently when the three of them were on shore, sitting on the veranda of an hotel on the seafront, waiting for the boat to Port Swettenham to take them to Sanpell's place. "Don't look so worried. I'll be all right after—after I get over the first shock. It isn't as though I'm alone. I've got Philip."

Morgan stared down into the lovely, tear-wet eyes.

"Yes, Lois, I know. But—"

He stopped, it was difficult to talk to Lois with Sanpell beside them. If only he could see her alone—tell her that he wanted her always to look on him as a friend. . . .

"I feel I must see you again, Lois. When Dick was dying, he asked me to—to sort of take his place—to always look after you. I'd like you to remember that I swore I would, Lois."

The tears rushed to her aching eyes.

"Of course I'll remember."

"It's very nice of Morgan, but you won't want anybody to look after you now you're my wife," said Philip rudely.

She flushed.

"Oh, of course not. But—Jimmy and I are old friends."

Philip hummed a little tune under his breath. This conversation was annoying him intensely. He felt his temper rising. He gained his feet and held out a hand to Lois.

"Come, darling," he said. "We'll get on board now."

She tried to smile through her tears. She looked a trifle wistfully at Jimmy. She would have liked to linger . . . hear more about her brother's death. It seemed as though Philip were taking her to alien

20

lands . . . to a new, strange home . . . and that in spite of her love for him she would be lonely and homesick . . . for, after all, she had not known him a very long time. Jimmy Morgan was part of the old, happy days.

Morgan stared down at Lois in miserable silence. The wistful look in her eyes haunted him. He realised how much he cared for her. . . . And she was going away with her husband . . . her husband . . . this big, handsome, ill-tempered brute!

"Good-bye, Lois," he said, pressing her hand. "And if ever you want me . . . I shall be in Kuala Lampor, myself, in a week's time."

"Oh, will you?" her voice was intensely glad. "But why?"

"I'm giving up the other estate now Dick is gone," he explained. "Some time back a fellow in K.L. named Williams asked me to join him. Also, I'm expecting my sister—you remember my young sister, Peggy?— out next week. She was asked out for a long stay with Williams and his wife."

"That will be nice," said Lois. "I'd like to see Peggy again—and you. Good-bye Jimmy."

"Good-bye, and I'm sorry I had to meet you with such news, Lois," he said huskily.

Half an hour later Lois was on board the little coasting steamer on its way to Port Swettenham. Up till now her thoughts had been so engrossed with sorrowful memories of Dick that she had not noticed that Philip had maintained a sulky silence since they had left Singapore. But now she became aware that he was silent, and that his handsome face was set, unfamiliar to her.

"Philip," she said timidly. "What is it, dear?"

He turned and looked at her. There was such a

strange look in his eyes that it made her feel hot, then cold. He said in a furious voice:

"I'd like to make it quite plain to you, Lois, that now you're my wife, you stick to me and my friends. I shall not allow you to keep up any tom-fool friendship with that fellow, Morgan, when he comes to K.L. You understand?"

Her heart gave a twist. She stared at him dumbfounded.

"But Philip—Jimmy was Dick's friend and—"

"I don't want to argue with you," he interrupted.

"Philip!" she said aghast.

With a savage little movement he caught her in his arms and pressed his lips against her soft mouth.

"You're mine, my wife now," he said in a low, fierce voice. "I won't have Morgan or any other fellow round you. You're mine, mine, Lois, and don't forget it!"

She was speechless . . . too astounded by his unreasonable attitude to attempt to argue. She only knew that she had never seen this side of Philip before and it terrified her. Could this bully really be the delightful, charming lover who had implored her to marry him on board? Oh, how little she knew about him! Dick was dead and she was going away to a strange home, a new life, and she belonged to Philip. Yes, he was emphasising that point fiercely. She belonged to him.

For the first time since she had known him, Lois did not thrill in response to Philip's ardent kisses and passionate arms. She hid her white face on his shoulder and trembled....

Philip was almost aggressively cheerful and buoyant during the drive in his car from Port Swettenham to Kuala Lampor. He took no notice of his wife's silence and—so it seemed to her—callously ignored her sorrow over her brother's untimely death.

"We'll drop in at the Club for a drink," Philip told Lois, "you meet everybody in K.L. at the Club. You must learn to enjoy a stinger or a suku . . . a stinger's a half-whisky and soda; suku's a quarter-whisky and soda."

She tried to smile. But she was nearer tears. It hurt her that Philip did not understand that she had not the least desire to stop at the Club and be introduced to a crowd of people. She was so sorely in need of solitude just now . . . of her husband's tenderness and sympathy.

She found herself, however, late that afternoon, seated on the veranda of the Club. Philip had said that he wanted to introduce her to his pals. But from the moment they had reached the Club he had vanished. . . . She had seen one or two men hail him and drag him to the bar . . . one or two women, too.

She sat alone feeling intensely depressed. If only Jimmy were not quite so far away. She was glad . . . yes, she was glad he was coming to Kuala Lampor. Whatever Philip said, she would not break her friendship with Dick's best friend.

Philip seemed to be away a long time. Lois grew restless and walked into the Club. Philip was not in the lounge. She wondered where he could be. She walked down a corridor, and came to a sort of smoking-room, the door of which was half ajar. She paused, rooted to the ground with amazement.

She had found Philip. He was standing in the centre of that room with a woman in his arms . . . a thin, red-haired woman in a white tennis frock with a

23

white Lenglen bandeau about her head. She was leaning back in a position of abandon and Philip's lips were against her throat.

Lois, hot and sick with shame, heard his voice:

"You see, I've still got a weakness for you, Lulu. No—of course I haven't forgotten last summer. But I had to get married sometime. It won't make much difference to us. Lois is an innocent sort of kid. She won't know...."

"I bet she doesn't know the first thing about you," interrupted the woman named Lulu. "I like your brand of kisses Phil, old thing, but I wouldn't live with you for long. You're too beastly bad-tempered."

Then they both saw the slim, hazel-eyed girl outside the door. They sprang apart. The red-haired woman gave an uneasy laugh and smoothed back her hair. Philip swore under his breath.

"That's done it. Well, so long, Lulu—see you sometime, I expect."

He turned from her and marched up to Lois; took her arm.

"For God's sake don't stand there looking so idiotic," he said rudely. "Come on. Let's get to the bungalow."

He half-led, half-dragged Lois out of the Club and pushed her into his waiting car. He spat out an order in Malay to the grinning syce at the wheel. The car moved off. Lois sat back staring blindly before her. Philip glanced at her.

"Come on, get it out, Lois,—say what you want to," at length he muttered.

She turned and looked at him. There was such heart-broken disillusion in her eyes that it would have made most men ashamed of themselves. But

Philip Sanpell did not know the meaning of shame. Lois said in a low, trembling voice :

"Philip . . . Philip . . . that woman . . . and you . . . oh, Philip ! "

"My dear girl, I knew her years before I met you. Her name's Louise Dickson . . . known as Lulu. Very good sort, even if her reputation is in shreds. She was divorced last year by old Ted Dickson who's in rubber out here. I used to be rather keen about her."

Lois sat rigid. She felt unable to answer. Her castle of dreams and romance crashed in ruins about her. And the prince of her dreams—Philip whom she had adored—was stripped of his mask. The real Philip was being revealed to her.

She covered her face with her hands and sat shuddering. For not only in this black hour did she realise that she no longer loved or respected Philip and had made a terrible mistake in marrying him; but she realised that she wanted Jimmy. It was Jimmy she had wanted all the time; Jimmy whom she knew was clean and honest and decent . . . and would have died before he humiliated or hurt her like this.

Her heart seemed to burst with shame and sorrow. She was Philip Sanpell's wife and she had discovered her love for Jimmy. It was so much too late.

Presently the car drew up before a big white bungalow and Philip said :

"Here we are, you foolish baby—here's your lord and master's home."

She was as white as parchment, and the frightened throb of her heart seemed to shake her slender body from head to foot.

The bungalow looked a palatial residence : large, cool and inviting; built on piles, and surrounded by a wide veranda. Two Malay boys stood on the steps respectfully waiting to greet their master.

Philip put an arm round Lois and led her into the living-room.

"Isn't this nice?" he said.

She looked about her. It was a nice enough room. Philip was fond of luxury. There were plenty of soft-cushioned chairs; a big divan; a gramophone brought out from England; a case full of books and big bowls of brilliant flowers everywhere.

From the windows Lois could see an attractive garden full of scarlet flowers which Philip said were cannias. And there were tall palms; deep, green, restful; and pale, grey rubber-trees.

"You'll find a bedroom prepared for us upstairs," said Philip. "I cabled to my boy to get it ready. I'm just going out to say a word to my head boy. I'll be back in a tick."

He vanished, and Lois walked slowly upstairs, a Malay following her, carrying two suitcases.

She shivered, in spite of the intense heat, as she walked into the bedroom to which the boy led her. She stood looking round her, slowly taking off her hat and smoothing back her hair which clung damply to her hot forehead. It was a pleasant bedroom; large, airy; a huge mosquito-cage built right round a large double divan bed with a coloured Egyptian cotton spread.

"Tuanada like some hot water to wash?" asked the Malay boy, who spoke tolerable English.

"Yes, please," began Lois. Then she paused, transfixed. Suddenly a long, wailing cry broke the stillness of the afternoon. Again came that cry . . . then another and another.

Lois rushed to the window. Her gaze fell on the tall figure of Philip down in the compound. He was quite close to the bungalow. She could see him plainly, and it seemed to her that his face was the face of the devil. It was convulsed with rage. At his feet a girl was kneeling. She was a slender Malay girl with dark, plaited hair and a handsome dusky face. She was clutching at Philip's arm. He, to Lois's horror, was beating her cruelly with a long piece of cane. The girl kept on wailing, clutching at him.

Lois staggered a little. She turned round to the boy; her eyes suffused; her cheeks colourless.

"Who is that girl. . . ?" The words escaped her quivering lips.

The Malay boy eyed her uneasily.

"Girl called Lalla . . . she begging Tuan (master) not to send her away now new Mem has come."

Now new Mem has come . . . the words sank into Lois's brain. What did that mean? The girl Lalla, what had she been, here, in this bungalow, to Philip?

She looked wildly around her. And gradually she noticed significant things. A pair of tiny, native woman's shoes beside the bed; a woman's kimono on the bed. The other thing was . . . a whip, hanging on the wall, close to the bed.

Lalla, the Malay girl whom Philip was so brutally beating in the compound, had lived in this bungalow with him; had shared this room with him. And she, Lois, the new Mem, was expected to sleep in that bed to-night. As for the whip . . . did Philip keep that whip in order to thrash women into submission?

A cry broke from her. She suddenly dropped her hat, turned, rushed past the astonished Malay boy out of the bedroom and down the stairs.

"Jimmy, Jimmy, save me . . . Jimmy. . . ."

She only got as far as the bottom of the garden, on the fringe of the rubber plantation, when Philip Sanpell caught her up. He had glimpsed that small, white flying figure and rushed after her.

As she felt his hands grip her shoulders, she gave a long piercing cry:

"Don't—don't . . . don't touch me . . . let me go!"

Sanpell held her fast, staring down at her convulsed face.

"What the devil's the matter, Lois? Where are you going?"

"Anywhere—anywhere," she sobbed hysterically. "But I won't stay with you."

"What do you mean?"

"I know," she said gasping. "I know what you are. That native girl Lalla . . . that whip . . . oh, you fiend!"

Light dawned on Philip Sanpell. He knew exactly what she meant and what had frightened her. He gave a low, scornful laugh.

"You little fool! That's nothing to do with you. That's my affair. As a matter of fact I meant Lalla to be out of the way when we got here. Anyhow, it's not your business. You belong to me. You're my wife, Lois, do you hear?—my wife! This is our wedding night!"

"But I won't live with you—I won't—I won't!" she screamed the words at him.

He lifted her right off her feet, laughing. He began to walk back to the bungalow, carrying her.

"Oh, won't you? We shall see, my child. I was going to put that whip away when you came, but it seems I'd better keep it out—for you."

She screamed again. Then her voice died away. Philip's lips were on her mouth, hotly, passionately . . . stifling her cries. She fainted dead away as he walked with her into the bungalow.

Early next morning Lois opened her eyes to see the pale, gold light of the rising sun slanting through the chinks in the green rush blind that hung over the three long windows in her bedroom.

For a few moments she lay still; half drowsing. Then she became conscious of a sharp pain in her head. Her temples seemed to throb as though from the dull pounding of a little hammer. The atmosphere in the big bedroom was very close. It was the beginning of a fiercely hot day in Kuala Lampor.

Then the stupor left Lois. She became wide-awake. Every nerve in her slim body tingled and quivered. She looked round the room with dilating eyes; then at the pillow beside her own. It bore the impress of a head—Philip's head.

But Philip had gone. She remembered now vaguely that she had heard him get up and dress and tell her that he was going to ride over the estate and "beat up the damned boys!"

To find him gone, to be alone in this room, was such a relief to Lois, that she flung herself face downwards on the pillows and began to cry, quietly, wretchedly.

She was remembering so many other things. Her whole body shook with the shame and despair of memories . . . of all the things that had happened since her husband had followed her last night; picked her up and brought her back to this bungalow. Since

29

then she seemed to have passed through a succession of nightmares ...

She looked back ... back to that moment when the scream of the Malay girl, Lalla, had reached her ears and she had seen Philip thrashing her ... and she had asked herself dully, why she had ever imagined herself in love with Philip Sanpell; why she had been so mad as to mistake a fleeting infatuation for genuine love. At the same time she saw the futility of her action in running away. She could not run away. Philip had caught her; Philip would always catch her and bring her back. He would never let her go. Last night he had said that it amused him to master her; to break her to his will. So he would keep her, here ... for his amusement.

She shuddered and ceased to cry ... just lay there, eyes shut ... body quivering. She thought of Jimmy. Ah, that thought was too agonising to bear. She could not have faced Jimmy this morning. In some dim way she felt beaten ... utterly ashamed. She just wanted to be alone.

At any moment Philip would be back to breakfast. The blood rushed hotly to her face as she thought of him, marching unceremoniously into this room. He would tease her, jeer at her because she had been crying.

Swiftly she got out of bed, put on a kimono, and pressed the bell next to her bed with a shaking little hand. That hand touched the whip near the bell. She drew away from it, her teeth clenching; turned from it shivering. That whip ... how dared he keep it there? It was an insult ... beyond pardon. He had not used it as he had threatened. That was because she had been beyond fighting him. But if she chose to fight, to argue, he might use it. A whip . . . on her . . . instead of Lalla. Something in Lois, some spirit yet unbroken by Philip Sanpell—rose in fierce revolt. Tearless, she stared at her reflection in the dressing-table mirror. She thought:

"I won't belong to him body *and* soul. My soul is my own—my heart, too, they will never belong to him—never!"

The bedroom door opened. She swung round, catching the kimono to her with a little gesture of terror that was tragic.

Philip walked in. He was extraordinarily good to look at. He carried his splendid head high. He was smiling. He looked proud and pleased, as though he had done some excellent work.

He looked at his wife.

"Oh, hullo—up, are you? I heard you ring. Want something?"

"My—bath," she stammered.

"I'll tell the boy to turn one on for you. To-morrow you'll have an amah to look after you," he said carelessly. "Hurry up, Lois, I want my breakfast. I'm devilish hungry."

"Yes," she said.

He glanced at her as he lit a cigarette; saw how the small, slender figure in the blue and white kimono was shuddering; saw that her hazel eyes were fixed on him; wide, bright with loathing. He knew then how utterly she hated him. It roused a demon in him. He walked up to her, put a hand on the nape of her neck, brushed up her fair, ruffled hair.

"Love me, baby?" he asked with superb insolence.

She said:

"Philip . . . I beg you. . . ."

"Oh, I don't want to kiss you," he said, and flung her away from him viciously. "Get dressed. I want something to eat."

Later she walked into the dining-room and found her husband eating a hearty breakfast of bacon and eggs and coffee. He glanced up at her. She looked extraordinarily fragile and sweet in a white linen dress with a scarlet patent-leather belt round the slim hips. Like a child. But her face was not the face of a child. The hazel eyes were the eyes of a woman in torment. The man who had done her such wrong frowned a trifle uneasily and looked away from her.

"Come on, Lois," he said gruffly. "Eat some of this food. It's good. The boys make good coffee."

"I'll have some coffee, thank you," she said.

"And some eggs and bacon."

"No—thanks."

"Rubbish—you can't starve," he said irritably. "Eat this."

He pushed a plate across the table to her. One of the boys in spotless white, his copper-coloured face impassive, poured her out a cup of coffee. Without speaking, she drank the hot liquid gratefully. But she could not touch the eggs and bacon. She felt sick.

Philip began to bully her.

"I won't have you starving yourself—just to spite me—just because you know I want you to eat."

"Oh, Philip—it isn't that at all," she protested flushing. "I—just don't want any."

Philip got up from the table and came round to Lois's side.

"If you won't eat, I shall feed you," he said. "There'll be no starvation business if I know it."

"Philip—please!" her eyes entreated him. "With

32

that native boy in the room,—you can't—"

"I shall do what I want in my own bungalow, and if the boy is watching us, all the better. I'll show him I'm master of my own wife." Philip put the knife and fork in her hands.

"Go on—eat it up," he added.

"You're treating me like—like a child," she said in a stifled voice, her face burning hot. "It's intolerable!"

But she ate the food. Anything rather than let Philip force it down her throat—with that brown-faced Malay boy watching inquisitively. At last she got up and escaped from the dining-room on to the veranda.

Philip followed her, whistling.

"Now perhaps you won't try to starve any more," he said. "What are you going to do with yourself this morning?"

"I don't know. Except that I'd like to be—left alone."

"Indeed!" he drawled. His temper had subsided. His faultless face was good-humoured again. He strolled up to his young wife and circled her with an arm. He ignored the fact that she shrank from him immediately.

"You'll find me much nicer if you'll only be nice, Lois, you pretty thing," he murmured. "Now kiss me —put your arms around me."

He swung her against him and crushed her lips down in a long kiss. She neither struggled nor spoke, but when he released her she was as white as her dress. His mood changed. He became irritable again. "It's like kissing a bit of ice. What a bride for a fellow! And you said you adored me."

"Philip," said Lois in a low voice, "I think there's a

33

demon—a cruel demon in you. You know that I did adore you—yes, and believed in you. But you know all that has happened since . . . to alter my feelings."

Moodily he tapped his riding boots with a crop.

"I don't believe it's me that's altered you at all. I believe it's that infernal fellow, Morgan."

Jimmy's name brought a red stain to her cheeks.

As she did not answer, Philip went on.

"Dishing up the old river-romance, what? Well, my dear little wife, you'll make a mistake if you try to weave romances round Morgan. I dislike the fellow, and I won't have him here."

Lois remained silent. She felt it impossible to reply. But, if anything, her contempt for this man she had married increased. The thought of Jimmy brought a red-hot throb of misery to her heart. She would have liked to have known that Jimmy was near—somewhere near—even though she could not have faced him this morning.

Finally Philip marched off to the bottom of the garden, where a boy waited with his chestnut mare. His final words to Lois were:

"You needn't try to run away, or do anything ridiculous. Kuala Lampor isn't a big place and I'd soon find out where you were. You can stay in the bungalow this morning while I'm on the estate. This afternoon you can put a pretty frock on and come to the Club."

The Club! Lois's lips twisted a little bitterly as she thought of the Club. She would have to meet Mrs. Dickson there again, no doubt. And others of Philip's friends who could never possibly become hers. No, she did not want to put on a pretty frock and be dragged to the Club.

34

Then it struck Lois, suddenly, that she might see Jimmy there; or at least Jimmy's sister, Peggy, who was staying in K.L. with the Williams's. Her sore, tired little heart gave a faint leap of hope. To see Jimmy . . . or Peggy . . . friends from home. That would be some comfort,—some happiness.

It seemed a long, lonely morning in the bungalow before Philip came back from his estate. Lois spent some of the time in unpacking her trunks; some in trying to comprehend the domestic workings of this strange, new home in Malaya, in trying to speak to the boys—give certain orders—to endeavour in a pathetic fashion to establish herself as mistress of the place.

But it seemed to Lois that there was always a covert, half-contemptuous smile behind the deference with which the boys treated her. And she knew—remembered with burning indignation and shame—that Lalla, the Malay girl who had lived here before her, was still here—in the compound,—sullen, yet perhaps hopeful that one day the Tuan would smile at her again.

From the very beginning the position for Lois was monstrous and intolerable.

CHAPTER II

AT five o'clock that afternoon the largest and most cosmopolitan club in Kuala Lampor was full of men seeking rest and recreation after the hot day's work, and women seeking diversion after an equally hot day of boredom. There is nothing for women to do in Malaya but to sit languidly about their bungalows waiting for late afternoon and the all-important cheerful gathering at the Club.

Lois Sanpell and her husband were a conspicuous couple on this particular afternoon. It was news indeed to everybody out here that "Handsome Philip" was married. Lois was stared at inquisitively. The men thought her adorably pretty, and much too young and innocent-looking for Sanpell with his devilish bad temper and nasty ways.

Many of the planters' wives had been out in Malaya two or three years without going home . . . many pairs of eyes were home-sick, wistful, as they rested on Lois's obviously new and fashionable dress from London town, and the delicate pallor of her face which had not yet got dried and brown—like theirs. They were nice to her; plunged into merry scandals of K.L. —invited her to their bungalows. But while Lois responded to these overtures and tried to be friendly and at her ease, she was acutely conscious of her secret terror and unhappiness at home; wondered what all these women who so admired her husband would say . . . if they knew.

Gradually the little crowd of polite, friendly

women drifted away from Lois. They thought her rather dull and awkward in spite of her prettiness. So she found herself quite alone on the veranda overlooking the tennis-courts. Philip was there, playing with Lulu Dickson; never once looking to see if his young wife were amused or happy. He did not seem to care.

Suddenly a bright, young voice behind Lois startled her out of her reverie.

"Lois—why, it's dear old Lois!"

She looked up quickly and saw a pretty girl in a pink linen dress, very short, showing graceful legs. One look at the brown bobbed head and dimpled cheeks and Lois sprang up with a cry of pleasure.

"Oh, Peggy—my dear—how nice!"

Jimmy Morgan's young sister flung herself into Lois's arms.

"Dear old thing—haven't seen you for years!"

Lois was horrified to find her eyes filling with tears . . . tears just because of a familiar face from England and a pair of intensely blue eyes so very like Jimmy's eyes. But she controlled her emotion and tried to speak gaily.

"I met Jimmy in Singapore. He told me you were out here. Sit down, Peggy—tell me all about yourself."

Peggy beckoned to a big, dark-haired man in white ducks, and a tall, slim girl with horn-rimmed spectacles.

"Let me introduce you, Lois. Mr. Williams—known as 'Tiny' because he's so big, and Mrs. Williams—Irene—who's a great friend of mine and has very kindly had me out here for a treat."

Lois shook hands with the Williams's. The party

sat on the veranda and ordered tea. Lois momentarily cheered up and talked and laughed with them. She had not seen much of Peggy in the old days. She was nineteen—six years younger than Jimmy—and had stayed once with Lois and Dick on the river. But Peggy was one of those friendly, merry girls who soon become intimate, and Mr. and Mrs. Williams were a delightful friendly pair, so Lois did not find it difficult to unbend.

Peggy—certainly neither subtle nor discerning— saw no tragedy lurking in the shadows of Lois's golden-hazel eyes and was swift to rhapsodise upon the fascination of Philip Sanpell.

"That tall man playing tennis—your husband? Heavens, Lois—how lucky you are—he's like a Greek God!" she exclaimed with her bubbling, infectious laugh.

"Yes, he is handsome," said Lois.

But "Tiny" Williams who had been some years in Malay, looked at Philip and gave an uneasy cough. Damn it, what hadn't he heard about the chap? Good lord . . . and married to this fragile golden-eyed little creature in the dark blue chiffon gown and floppy blue hat? . . . Lois looked a mere child!

Then Mr. and Mrs. Williams carried Peggy off to introduce her to some friend of theirs, and Lois found herself alone on the veranda again. She sat quietly watching Philip playing tennis with Lulu Dickson.

Then suddenly Jimmy Morgan walked into the Club, and the world seemed to spin round Lois. Through a kind of mist she saw his familiar figure step out of a car and walk up the veranda towards her.

"Oh,—Jimmy," she said, and held out her hands.

38

Jimmy Morgan grasped both those hands; looked down at her speechless for an instant. Then he said:

"Lois, my dear."

"How—why are you here? I never expected . . . such a surprise . . ." she stammered and stopped.

"Didn't Peggy tell you? Haven't you seen her yet? I wired her that I'd be in K.L. this afternoon and come straight along here. I thought I might see you, Lois. Everybody comes along here."

"Peggy didn't tell me. But I'm—so glad to see you, Jimmy."

Now that the first surprise of seeing him had passed, the hot, pink colour had also gone and left her deadly pale. Jimmy took the basket-chair beside her, unconscious that he still gripped her hands and was holding them tightly between his own. His gaze was riveted on her. He saw how altered she was. Unbelievably changed since their last meeting in Singapore. He looked at the tragic curve of her pretty mouth, at the pain in her eyes, and his heart gave a jerk.

"Oh, my dear, what has happened to you?"

She flushed again and drawing her hands from his, locked them nervously in her lap.

"Oh,—nothing."

"Lois," said Jimmy, "you can't deceive me. I know you too well. Oh, my darling, who has hurt you? You look . . . kind of broken . . ."

The word "darling" had slipped out unconsciously. Lois heard it and quivered. A pleasure so poignant that it became pain thrilled her from head to foot. But she could not meet his eyes. Her head drooped.

Jimmy, his brows knit, breathing fast, looked up and around him. Then he saw Philip Sanpell on the tennis courts. He had just finished a sett and was talking to Lulu Dickson across the net. Jimmy's lips tightened. He could see the bold, intimate way in which Lulu laughed up at Philip . . . and in a flash he knew what was wrong with Lois, knew that her marriage to Philip had been as disastrous as he had feared it would be.

"Lois," he said, "you're not happy with Sanpell!"

"I—oh, Jimmy—" she faltered helplessly. She did not know what to say. But she could not lie to Jimmy, with his very blue eyes penetrating into her mind. She knew, as she sat here beside him, that she loved him—needed him. It was a dreadful position.

Jimmy rose and held out a hand. He was pale under his tan.

"Lois, come indoors . . . there's a room . . . where we can get away from folk . . . be quiet a moment. I must talk to you."

She wanted to refuse; realised the danger of being alone with Jimmy. But the look in his eyes was insistent; and, after all the anguish, the disillusion, the broken love, she wanted so badly to turn to him—this man who had been her first sweetheart, who was the only one, really, in the world whom she could love.

She gave him her hand and passed with him into the club-house. They found a room, cool, deserted, green blinds shading it from the fierce sunlight, a room wherein one could play cards or read. But there was nobody in it now.

Jimmy put his hands on Lois's slender shoulders. He looked down at her with his searching eyes.

"Lois," he said, "don't hide things from me. My dear, I was Dick's best pal, and he asked me to take care of you when he—passed out. Lois, it's more than I can bear to see you looking so unhappy, so ill."

She shivered as though with cold. She whispered:

"I need you—your friendship—terribly; but don't ask me about Philip."

"I must ask. He isn't kind to you? Is that it?"

"Don't—Jimmy—"

"Lois," said Jimmy hoarsely, "you're dearer to me than any woman on earth—even Peggy, my little sister. If you need any help you must ask for it without being ashamed or afraid. At Singapore I guessed this would happen. It maddens me."

She looked at him with great, pitiful eyes.

"Jimmy—I—it was my fault—for marrying him. I was mad. But what can I do—now?"

He was answered. She was desperately unhappy with Sanpell, and regretted her marriage. He wondered what Sanpell had done to break her like this in so short a time. It rushed across him in a warm, living stream of light that he was more than her friend. He was her lover, who loved and adored her and would give his life to make her happy. And she belonged to Philip. . . .

"Lois," he said, "listen, my dear. I'm staying with Tiny Williams to-night, but to-morrow I go to my own bungalow, as I don't approve of sharing with young married folk like the Williams's. Later, Peggy may join me. But you must remember that my bungalow is only ten miles north from your place, and if you want me—"

He paused. He was aghast to see her crying. Great tears poured down her pale, little face. And at the sight of those tears his control snapped. He put both his arms round her and drew her to his heart.

"Oh, Lois, my little Lois! Oh, darling, darling, don't cry," he said.

She, too, was at breaking point. For a moment she clung to Jimmy. The warmth and comfort of his embrace was so very comforting. She had scarcely known, until she felt his arms enfolding her, how much she had loved this man.

"Jimmy—Jimmy," she whispered.

"Oh, Lois, my darling!" he groaned, and clasped her closer. How thin, how fragile she was—his poor little Lois! His lips brushed the velvet of her cheeks; the wet silk of her long lashes. Passion and pity shook him. Recklessly he held and kissed her as though he would never let her go. "I love you—I love you—oh, how I love you!" he kept on saying.

"I love you too, Jimmy. I've always cared. Oh, Jimmy I didn't realise what I was doing! I was mad and blind—to marry Philip. Oh, Jimmy what can we do now?"

The man suddenly pulled himself together. He was very conscious once more that Lois was Sanpell's wife. He had no right to kiss her, make love to her like this. He took her hands and laid his face against the little pink, cupped palms.

"Beloved, this is madness. I must be off my head. But I love you Lois, and it is more than flesh and blood can stand to know that you are so unhappy with Sanpell."

She was no longer a pale, timid, shrinking girl. She was an ardent-eyed woman who loved; who knew herself beloved. She looked up at Jimmy with starry eyes.

"My dear, I'm glad you told me—glad—glad that you love me."

"Oh, darling, darling!" he half-groaned, half-laughed. "What can I do? I oughtn't to see you again."

And then Philip Sanpell came into the room, noiselessly on his rubber-soled tennis shoes. Lois's heart leapt guiltily as she saw him. She moved away from Jimmy. What had he seen? How long had he been in the doorway? She could guess nothing from his expression. He was smiling affably. He even greeted Jimmy with a smile.

"How are you, Morgan? Baby darling, ready to get back home? Come along then. Goo'bye, Morgan."

He flung an arm carelessly about Lois. Jimmy saw her go white, but she moved away with her husband without a word. Jimmy was left alone in that room, torn, harassed, uncertain.

Philip maintained an apparently agreeable silence until he reached home with his wife. She had nothing to say. But her heart was shaking and her cheeks were on fire when she remembered Jimmy's mad, sweet kisses—her own response to his passion of love and longing. In some queer way the knowledge of their mutual love made her strong, roused the fighting spirit in her. She would not submit to Philip's brutalities without standing up to him—now that she was armoured by Jimmy's love.

But once they were alone in the big, cool living-room of their bungalow, Philip's savage temper flared up.

"What the hell did that fellow mean by kissing you, Lois?" he snarled. "I saw him—saw you in his arms—you little—"

"Be quiet, Philip," she broke in. She faced him

bravely although she trembled. "Don't dare insult me."

"Insult you? By God, that's good! And you fresh from Morgan's kisses! His bungalow's only ten miles away from here, is it? Going to protect you from me, is he? We'll see."

"Philip—be quiet."

Her firm little voice amazed him for a moment. She was going to stand up to him, was she? Morgan's love-making had changed her. She was no longer the shrinking, terrified creature she was last night. That enraged Philip Sanpell.

"We'll see whether your fine Jimmy can protect you or not," he said, livid with fury. "We'll see whose kisses you prefer . . . his or mine . . . when I've finished with you, my child."

Her heart shook, but she held her head erect.

"Philip—you have no right to speak to me like this."

"What you think and what I think are two different things," he said savagely. He strode across the room to her and caught her in his arms. He gave a low, cruel laugh, as he saw her flinch and whiten. "You like Mr. Jimmy's embraces and not mine, nowadays, eh? I'll teach you to flirt, Lois. I'm dam' well going to lock you in this bungalow when I'm out of it. I'll see you don't get a chance to run whining to Morgan's bungalow."

His arms crushed and hurt her. His fingers tore a piece of the delicate, blue chiffon of her frock.

"Philip, Philip, let me go! Oh, you coward, you bully, haven't you punished me enough already?"

"No—not nearly enough," he said. His face was convulsed with dark passions. "You hate me now,

44

don't you, eh? Hate me!"

"Yes—I do—I hate you!" she said, wildly struggling in his arms. "Let me go—I do hate you—you brute—you beast!"

"Ah, that's good!" he laughed and flung her away from him. "Well, Lalla used to hate me sometimes. And I used to thrash her until she crawled into my arms and begged me to let her love me again. I'll treat you like I'd treat a Malay girl, my charming wife, who would run away to Mr. Morgan's bungalow if she could. . . ."

Lois lay on the floor where he had thrown her. Her fair hair was hanging over her brows, her cheeks livid. She was terrified. Brave though she was, Philip was so much stronger physically. And when he marched back into the room, carrying that dreadful whip in his hand, she suddenly sprang to her feet and rushed wildly to the window. She shrieked and shrieked aloud.

"Jimmy—Jimmy—help me—help!"

At that moment a car stopped outside Sanpell's bungalow, and a man stepped out of it and began to walk slowly up to the front door.

Jimmy Morgan disliked coming to Sanpell's place. But in the excitement of meeting Lois this afternoon at the Club he had forgotten to give her a small packet which he had found in Dick's kit at Singapore; a little box of precious stones which he knew Dick had been collecting for his sister. So Jimmy, remembering the packet after Lois had gone, had decided to drop it at Sanpell's place, on his way to the Williams's bungalow.

Reaching the bungalow, he heard a shrill, agonised scream—the scream of a woman in pain. He stopped.

He recognised Lois's voice. It was Lois who was screaming. She was calling:

"Jimmy— Jimmy— Jimmy—help me!"

Jimmy took two flying leaps; one on to the veranda, the other in through the mosquito-netting door which led into the living-room.

"Lois!" he shouted. "Lois, where are you? I'm here...."

He paused on the threshold of the living-room. For an instant he stood rigid, appalled by what he saw.

On a rug in the centre of the room a girl was crouching. . . a little, slender, shivering girl, with a dead white face and great eyes dilated with terror. It was Lois . . . Lois with her blue chiffon gown torn in shreds; one white shoulder bare, showing a red mark right across the marble whiteness. Lois, moaning and writhing under the sharp lash of a whip. Standing over her, and holding her by one wrist, was the man who wielded the whip—Philip Sanpell. His face was convulsed, the face of a devil rather than a man.

Lois saw Jimmy and tried to wrench her hand away from her husband.

"Oh, Jimmy, Jimmy . . . save me!" she moaned.

Jimmy sprang . . . his mind seething with the most passionate fury he had ever known in his life. He sprang straight at Sanpell . . . at the man's throat.

"You swine—you damn beast!" he said between his teeth.

Jimmy was by nature a peaceful, placid young man, not given to rows or violence. But the sight of Lois—the woman he loved and for whom he would have died—being brutally thrashed was more than he could stand.

Philip dropped the whip and his wife's wrist as

46

Jimmy so unexpectedly sprang at him. He gave a snarling laugh and locked with the other man.

"Oh, ho," he said, "Lois's champion, eh? We'll see...."

Lois who had fallen forward, half fainting, roused herself to full consciousness and staggered to her feet. She pulled the torn pieces of chiffon about her shoulders, her dilated eyes riveted on the two men who were now grappling with each other. She sobbed under her breath as she watched them.

The cruel whipping which she had received had unnerved her. But she was brave—there was a spirit in her that not even Sanpell's cruelty could bury. Moving away from the two men she watched them breathlessly. She did not look at Philip—she could not bear the sight of his demoniac features. But she looked at Jimmy, and something in her thrilled at the sight of him. Jimmy, her beloved! Ah, he was a champion of whom any woman could be proud. He was gradually weakening Sanpell, who was of slimmer build and without a quarter of Jimmy's stamina.

Soon a hoarse cry burst from Philip.

"Stop it, you fool—you're breaking my back!"

Lois's terrified eyes left Jimmy for an instant—turned to her husband. She saw to her horror that Philip was being bent completely backwards by the weight of Jimmy's great body and the force of his fingers round his throat. Philip's face was a purplish hue; his eyes were bulging; his body looked horrible to Lois, curved backwards like that. She rushed forward.

"Jimmy—don't kill him!"

"I'd like to," said Jimmy incoherently. "I'd like to kill him...."

And then Philip turned his bulging eyes upon the young wife whose heart he had broken . . . and he whined to her.

"Lois—tell him to let me go—I'm sorry—oh, he's going to break my spine! . . ."

Lois shuddering, touched Jimmy's shoulder.

"Please—it isn't worth it—let him go—"

Jimmy released Philip who staggered back, cursing and coughing. But Jimmy had not finished with him yet.

"Lois—leave us, get out of the room, my dear," he said. He was still blind with fury. "I haven't given this beast half enough punishment yet. I won't kill him—don't worry, dear. But he's going to taste the whip he used on you!"

Lois stared at him speechless. His blue eyes softened; his whole face grew tender as he looked down at her piteous little face.

"Go, dear," he said gently. "Pease—quickly."

Lois stumbled out of the room. She heard her husband fling an oath at Jimmy as she went . . . heard Jimmy say:

"Now you wife-beater—let's see how you like the whip. . . ."

More oaths from Philip . . . a crack of a whip . . . the sharp howl of the man upon whom it landed.

Lois felt deadly sick. She put her hands to both ears and stumbled to her bedroom. She could not listen to those sounds any more. It was all too horrible; too revolting.

The world seemed to spin round her for a few moments. She managed to reach her bed and lay down on it, face buried in the cool linen of the pillow. She lay motionless until her feeling of nausea passed.

Her shoulders ached and throbbed where the whip had raised weals. Her head seemed on fire.

How long she lay there with closed eyes and every nerve bruised and quivering, she knew not. But after awhile she became aware that someone was in the room. She looked up and saw a native woman in the doorway; a strange woman in a white, loose coat and sarong, with a flat, yellowish face and oily black hair done in a tight knob at the back of her head. She smiled and bowed when Lois looked up at her.

"Good-day, Mem."

"Who are you?" asked Lois.

"I am amah . . . Tuan sent for amah to wait on Tuanada."

Lois understood. This was the high-class Chinese nurse whom Philip had engaged for her. She was a woman of thirty-five or forty; looked quite pleasant and clean and spoke quite good English; had obviously been in some English family before this. But Lois did not want the amah just now. She was proud and fastidious. It was more than she could tolerate to allow an amah to see her lacerated shoulder and torn frock; let the woman realise what the Tuan had done.

"You can come to me later, amah," she said, hastily lying back on the bed so as to hide her dishevelled dress. "I don't want you now."

"Very good, Mem," said the woman, and departed, having first thrown a curious, inquisitive look round the room and at the white lady.

When the amah had gone, Lois closed her eyes again and tried desperately to pull herself together. What was Jimmy doing to Philip, now? What would Philip do, after this? She dared not think.

Then Jimmy Morgan opened the bedroom door.

"Lois—may I come in?"

"Yes," she said under her breath.

He came in and stood beside her bed. He was flushed and breathless and his lips were a grim line, but the blue eyes that looked down on the girl were very tender.

"You poor little darling," he said. "Oh, Lois I am glad I dropped in! It was only by pure accident . . . I had a packet for you from Dick which I had forgotten to give you at the Club. When I saw that brute hitting you, I could have shot him. I believe I would have shot him if someone had put a gun into my hands."

Lois's golden eyes filled with hot tears which welled over and ran down her cheeks.

"I'm glad you did come Jimmy. But he—isn't worth shooting."

"You're right," said Jimmy grimly. "Well, he's had a taste of that whip he's so fond of. He's lying on the floor of the living-room now cursing the day he was born and vowing vengeance on me."

She shuddered and turned her face to the pillow. "Jimmy . . . it's terrible, frightful. . . ."

He knelt down by the bed and put an arm about her. It was terrible to see her lying on that bed; sick, shivering, physically tortured by Sanpell.

"Lois," he said, "this would have broken old Dick's heart. I am glad he isn't here to see."

"So—am—I," came from Lois in a muffled voice. "Oh, Jimmy what can I do?"

"You must leave him—at once," said Jimmy in a very decided voice.

She looked up at him.

"I'd like to. But I don't see how I can."

"You must come to me, Lois."

Her tear-wet face burned.

"How can I, Jimmy! I am Philip's wife."

"He's forfeited his right to you, Lois, after what he has done."

"I don't think the law would release me from my contract—because he's hit me—once," she said bitterly. "Remember, Jimmy, I've only been married a few days."

"You can't stay here in this bungalow and be subjected to his brutality," said Jimmy. "I couldn't rest, day or night, for thinking of you here, Lois."

Her arms went blindly round his neck. "Oh, Jimmy, Jimmy . . . what could I do without you, now?"

He held her close, his lips on her silky fair hair.

"Sweetheart . . . oh, my poor little Lois . . . if only you had married me instead of him."

"If only I had!" she echoed the words, the tears streaming down her face. Then as Jimmy tightened his hold of her she winced. He saw her whiten, and gave a shocked exclamation.

"Your back . . . my dear . . . oh, let me see—did he hurt you badly, my darling?"

She tried to laugh. "It's nothing. . . ."

But Jimmy rolled her gently over in the bed and saw the livid, angry weals on the velvet whiteness of her shoulder. The sight made him seethe with rage, but he said quietly:

"Darling child—let me bathe it—see to it for you."

She said in a shamed voice: "No—I can manage myself—only I don't want that Chinese woman . . . the amah, to touch me . . . realise what has happened. Jimmy darling, you must go, I'll see to the back myself. It isn't so bad."

Her courage made his heart ache for her.

"Oh Lois, dear, dear little Lois, I can't leave you alone in the bungalow with that fiend."

"You must Jimmy . . ." For an instant she leaned her tired head against his heart—clung to him with passion. "I love you, you know that. But I can't forget that I am Philip's wife. Perhaps it is my duty to stick to him, to try to pull him round. Perhaps after this he'll mend. I ought to give him a chance anyhow. I think what you've done will do him some good."

For a moment Jimmy did not speak. The fine courage and honour of this girl who had been so terribly disillusioned in her marriage, was something marvellous. He bent and kissed her, with more reverence than passion, between her eyes.

"My dear," was all he could say.

"You understand, don't you, Jimmy?"

"Absolutely, darling. You're too good for me. But you've got to remember that I do truly love and adore you, Lois, and if you want me . . . if things get too bad for you here, you must come to me."

"I'll remember," she whispered. She smiled bravely up at him . . . held out her right hand. "You must go now Jimmy. Whatever we do we mustn't give Philip a chance to accuse us."

Jimmy kissed the small hand.

"I hate leaving you . . . with him, Lois."

"I'll be all right. I lost my nerve just now, when he . . . hit me . . ." she swallowed hard. "But I've got it back, and I can tackle him, myself, now. After all, I married him, and I've got to abide by my choice, and not weakly slink out of it."

"You're wonderful, Lois," said Jimmy. "I'll go. I'm glad I thrashed the swine. Dearest, if you want me

. . . send to me . . . or come . . . to my bungalow . . . at once."

She nodded mutely. He pulled himself together and walked from the room . . . out of the bungalow.

Philip Sanpell did not face his wife that night. Nor for many nights.

He was a peculiar man, and one of his peculiarities was a terrific aversion to loss of dignity. The thrashing Jimmy Morgan had given him had not only cut his shirt to ribbons, marked his flesh and bruised his face, but taken away his dignity. An exceptionally handsome man, in his normal sane moods, he was used to admiration. He could not have borne to stay in his bungalow, wincing at the pain on his shoulders or showing a black eye and cut lip to his servants. He also felt he would be in an ignominious position with Lois if he stayed. He had been a beast and brute to her. He knew it. He bitterly resented Morgan's interference, but he knew he had deserved what he had got.

He was not going to face Lois and home life again until he had regained superiority and dignity. So he just cleared out . . . for the time being . . . flung a few clothes into a suitcase, took his car and departed for Port Swettenham, whence he took the boat for Singapore. In Singapore there were places known to Philip where he could hide until his back had healed and his face was normal again. He went to one place —the sort that most white men avoid, but to which Philip was no stranger . . . and where there was a Spanish girl who had loved him for years; on whose kisses and consolation he could depend.

During that week Lois hung about the bungalow,

nerving herself for the next meeting with her husband, and glad in her heart that he had gone. She had no car. Philip had taken that. She could not get into town or see people like Peggy Morgan or the Williams's, and none of the women had begun to pay calls yet. So she spent that week entirely alone day and night.

She did not know where her husband was. He had only left word with the house-boy that he had "gone away on business". The scene she had anticipated had not come off. But she felt very uneasy about things; felt as though this was only the calm preceding the storm; and that Philip was bottling things up for her.

She could have sent for Jimmy . . . or gone to him. But although she longed passionately for his comfort, his companionship, she made no effort to see him. She felt it better not. She loved him so . . . it was hard to be strong when she was with him. She must remember that she was Philip's wife.

By the end of that week the weals on her back had healed. She only felt a little stiffness to remind her of that ignominious beating. She tried not to think of it; not to remember her husband with loathing and aversion. She did her utmost to school herself into a calm, forgiving mood; to greet him amicably when he returned.

She told herself that if she showed Philip a little love, a little tenderness—if she forgave him, she might win him round; drive that devil out of him. At any rate, she believed it her duty to try.

But as the days and nights wore on, she became more and more uneasy and the loneliness began to get on her nerves. She grew to hate the sight of the rubber-trees; of the whole, vast plantation. The heat

54

tried her sorely . . . the sandflies and mosquitoes were maddening.

Then suddenly late one evening she heard a car drive up to the bungalow. She went to the front door, her body quivering with nerves, her pale, thin little face expectant.

It was Philip.

He walked calmly into the bungalow, followed by the white-coated boy who carried his suitcase. He was perfectly normal again. There was no mark of violence on his handsome face. He was extremely pale, and the brilliant dark eyes were ringed with shadows. But he had regained his dignity, at least, in his own imagination. He could walk firmly and gracefully again. He would not have to creep about the place groaning and whining.

He looked at his young wife with inscrutable eyes. She gave him a timid, appealing little smile and said:

"I'm glad you're back, Philip."

Any ordinary man would have been touched. He had thrashed her, terrified her, and she greeted him charmingly. But Philip was not touched. Under his calm exterior—the cool mask he adopted this evening —he seethed with the old longing to hurt her; break her. And still more deadly was his passion of resentment against Lois's old friend, Morgan, who had dared to punish him. One day Morgan should suffer. But now he was going to deal with Lois.

He gave her a smile that was encouraging.

"Hello, Lois," he said. "Had supper?"

"Yes."

"Well, I'll just have a bite, then we'll sit on the veranda and talk. I've been away rather longer than I expected. Business at Singapore. How are you, Baby?"

She murmured some reply. As she followed him into their bedroom her heart-beats quickened . . . shook her slender body . . . her face flamed and paled and flamed again. Uneasily she looked at her husband's handsome face. How extraordinary he was. How difficult to understand! He spoke and behaved as though that terrible scene with Jimmy had never taken place. He treated her in a casual, ordinary fashion . . . just as any husband might return to any wife after a spell of absence . . . he seemed to ignore the fact that the last time he had seen her he had cruelly ill-treated her.

He was brushing his sleek, dark hair in front of her mirror now, chatting amiably to her. But, she could not, somehow, feel at ease. There had been something queer, inscrutable in his smile, in his eyes, when he greeted her.

Suddenly he walked up to her and caught her roughly in his arms.

"You pretty thing—are you really glad to see me back?"

She bit her lip nervously. The clasp of his arms revolted her. Somehow she could not respond to his embraces now . . . after all that had happened. She looked up at the face which she had once thought the most handsome in the world, and seemed to see it convulsed with demoniac fury . . . as it had looked when he had whipped her. He felt her shiver and drew her closer; put a forefinger under her chin and lifted her face to his.

"Lois," he said, "you haven't been sulking all this time, harbouring malice against me, have you?"

"No," she faltered. "In a way I haven't, but Philip,

you must remember that it will be very difficult for me to forget—what you did."

His eyes narrowed. He kept her close.

"Equally difficult for me to forget what—your precious friend Morgan did to me."

She winced and tried to escape his hold.

"Philip, let's forget it all, for heaven's sake. It is so horrible. You—you must have been mad. That wasn't the real you."

"Oh, wasn't it?" He laughed . . . his dark eyes looked tormented; hungry . . . "And you want to be friends with me again do you, Lois?"

"Y-yes," she stammered. "Let's be friends."

"Lovers, too, eh?"

"Anything," she said bravely—"anything, if you will only—be different again, Philip—be—like you used to be on the boat."

The fragrance of her hair, the slenderness of her, the delicate whiteness of her, mounted to the head of the man who, for seven days and nights, had flung himself to a hell of dissipation in Malay Street, Singapore. He laid his flushed face against hers; ignored the fact that she shivered and shrank from him; began to kiss her with slow, deliberate kisses.

"My wife, Lois—still mine. We'll begin again—oh, yes!—and we'll not only wipe out the memory of that other night, but the existence of Mr. James Morgan. You'll never kiss him again, Lois. You'll just kiss me . . . like you used to on the boat."

He mimicked her voice. She could feel him sneering through all the mask of amiability; could feel that he was not genuine. He had not come back to beg her pardon, to reform, but only to hurt and torment her afresh. She tried to evade his kisses.

"Philip—Philip—be decent for once—let's talk things over—Philip—let me go!"

"Want to give me a lecture . . . reform me, darling? Well, I'd rather kiss you. You're so damned pretty," he laughed.

She struggled out of his arms and ran to the door. But Philip was there first. He locked the door and pocketed the key.

She sobbed helplessly as his arms went round her again and his lips closed on her mouth.

In the cold, grey light of dawn Lois made up her mind once and for all that she could not remain with Philip. All through the night he had tormented her, sneered at her regard for Jimmy, forced upon her the fact that she belonged to him, Philip, and destroyed any hopes that she might have cherished that he would be different, that her presence in the bungalow could soften and reform him.

Dawn found her up and dressed while Philip was still sleeping. She was quite calm and very determined. All the fighting spirit in her was roused. All her pride was in revolt.

She told the amah to pack her few clothes in the adjoining room where they could not rouse Philip; then ordered the syce to bring round the car.

"You will come with me, amah," she said to the Chinese woman. "I have left a message on my dressing-table for the Tuan."

"Yes, Mem," said the woman obediently.

Lois was going to Jimmy. In her extremity she turned to him quite naturally and simply. To whom else could she go? Who else had she in the world to turn to but Dick's friend?

58

She did not pause to wonder what Philip would do when he discovered that she had gone. She only wanted to get away . . . away from this dreadful, lonely bungalow, where she was utterly in the power of the man she had married.

The sun was just breaking through the pearl-grey clouds of the dawn when her car reached Jimmy's bungalow, a smaller dwelling that Sanpell's, with a rather neglected, straggling little garden.

But the first things Lois saw when she opened the door, followed by the amah (who was both servant and chaperon), were Jimmy's rocking chair, a magazine, a pipe and pouch on the veranda. Little homely touches speaking of him! She walked into the shabby little bungalow with the sensation that it was a palace compared to the luxurious place she had just left and where she had known so much agony, mental and physical.

Jimmy, roused from sleep by the sound of the car which was departing, hastened into the living-room. His curly hair was rough; tousled like a boy's; his eyes heavy with sleep. When he saw the forlorn little figure of Lois and the amah behind her, bearing her suitcase, he gave a cry of astonishment.

"Lois! What has happened, dear?"

"Philip came back last night after having been away a week," she said, quite quietly. "He was—vile, Jimmy. I can't stand any more. I've come to you."

Then she crumpled up at his feet. He picked her up, his heart pounding. Lois had come to him. That was all that seemed to matter. The seriousness of the step she had taken did not for the moment strike him.

He laid her on the sofa by the window and gave the amah a sharp order.

"The Tuanada has fainted. See to her. I am going to get some clothes on."

"Yes, Tuan," said the woman, in her laconical voice.

Lois's fainting fit passed quickly. Ten minutes later she was seated on the sofa at Jimmy's side, one hand locked fast in his, telling him everything.

The amah had retired to the servants' compound.

"You see, Jimmy," said Lois, "I just can't bear any more."

"No, by heaven, and why should you?" said Jimmy. By this time he had changed speedily into riding kit. "My dear, you don't know how happy I am that you have come to me."

"But now I've come—how can I stay," she said with a brief, tired laugh. "There is Philip to deal with yet."

"He must give you a divorce."

"I don't somehow think he will—even if I give him the—evidence." Lois's cheeks crimsoned.

Jimmy gripped her other hand, kissed them both passionately.

"My darling—you're a saint. It's he—that filthy brute—who ought to give you evidence."

"Somehow, I feel he won't—do either," said Lois in a frightened voice. "Jimmy, I don't know what it is—but some demon in Philip makes him want to master me. He'll never stop trying now."

"He won't get a chance to touch you again."

"But he won't set me free. Jimmy, Jimmy, we're in a very serious position," she cried. And suddenly she put both hands up to her head as though it hurt her. "Jimmy, this is going to be terrible."

Jimmy stood up, his face set and hard.

"I swear I'm going to protect you now, Lois," he said.

"But I'm—still—Philip's wife."

"I shall never rest until you are mine, Lois,"

She was silent. Here in this little, sun-lit living-room —so typically a bachelor's room—she could be happy and at peace. If only Life would let her be. But there was no peace now. The atmosphere was charged with terrors, difficulties, vibrant with men's passions. . . . So it seemed to Lois.

Suddenly Jimmy walked to the window.

"Now for a row, Lois," he said under his breath. "This is your car, and Sanpell's in it. He's come for you!"

CHAPTER III

"Jimmy," said Lois. "You won't let him take me!"

"Not I, darling," said Jimmy. "The devil himself couldn't take you from me if you want to stay."

Lois hid her face in her hands.

"I can't go back to him," she said.

Philip walked into the room and marched straight up to his wife.

"What the blazes are you doing in Morgan's bungalow?"

"Careful, Sanpell," broke in Jimmy. "We don't want a repetition of last week's affair."

Philip's lips curled into a sneer.

"You're being funny, Morgan. I reckon I've got good grounds for divorce over this."

"File your petition, then," said Jimmy. "I'm proud to stand by Lois as her protector."

"Protector!" Philip laughed. "Lover, you mean."

Lois moved in between the two men. They were glaring at each other; their faces white; their hands clenched.

"Jimmy—please go, my dear. Let me speak to Philip alone."

"Are you sure, Lois?" he began.

"Sure," she broke in. "Please, my dear."

He bit his lip. She had been through so much. He did not want to leave her to the mercy of Sanpell's vile tongue. But her eyes implored him to go. He turned and walked out of the room.

"I shall be on the veranda, if you want me, Lois."

Lois faced her husband, her head erect. But she was trembling. She went straight to the point.

"You know that I have never been unfaithful to you, Philip. But you have broken every vow you have made to me. You have made me loathe you. I am going to leave you, and I will never, never live with you again!"

Philip's eyes blazed, but he seemed to make an attempt to control himself.

"I see. So you loathe me and you mean to fly to the arms of Jimmy Morgan."

"He is my friend."

"You deny you are lovers?"

"I don't deny we love each other," she corrected. "But don't think because you have no honour, no principle, that everybody is the same. For my brother's sake, Jimmy would never hurt a hair of my head—let alone for my own sake."

"Really?" drawled Philip. "But how charming! So you are going to set up housekeeping together—platonically!"

Lois looked at her husband, her lips curling.

"What a beast—what a cad you are, Philip!"

"Do you think I believe in that drivel about platonic friendship between a pretty girl and a man?" he snarled. "No, I know too much about it."

"I shall stay with Jimmy, as a friend, until I can get back to England."

"With whose money?"

"That will be a difficulty," she admitted.

"I shan't finance your passage home," he said. "You can come back to me if you want to have my money."

"I would rather starve, Philip."

"And once you adored me. Come, come, Lois!"

"You killed my love."

"Well, it's your own fault. You're nothing but an icicle, damn it!"

Suddenly Philip's arms were about her.

"Lois, you can't hate me so. I haven't lost you for good and all, have I? Darling, come back to me. You'll break my heart if you won't!"

She looked at him and knew he no longer had power to stir her. Her love, even her pity for Philip was dead. She could not believe in him; could not forgive him. He had made her melt, surrender before, only to swing back to passion and cruelty again. She pushed him gently away from her.

"Don't Philip—let me go—I can't believe in you. I know you don't mean that you are sorry."

She sensed the hypocrite behind the ardent, repentant lover. She was no longer blinded by his sheer masculine beauty or magnetism. And when Philip realised that she stood firm, and that he could not drag or lure her back to him, he dropped his lover-like mask. He released her—pushed her rudely away from him.

"All right—go your own way and I'll go mine," he said savagely.

She looked at him through a film of tears.

"Can't you be decent—and set me free?"

"No—you can do what you like—go off with Morgan—leave Malaya with him—I don't care. I shall never divorce you so that you can marry him. You belong to me, and one day you shall come back to me, Lois."

He marched out of the room and slammed the door in her face. Lois walked to a chair and sat down . . . she put her face in her hands.

Jimmy came into the room. She felt his arms about her.

"Lois, my poor, poor, little Lois."

She clung to him, desperately.

"What shall we do, Jimmy? What shall we do?"

"God knows, darling. But we'll find some way out. Tell me everything that Sanpell said."

Jimmy and Lois talked for an hour. At the end of that hour they realised the difficulties facing them.

Jimmy was, comparatively, a poor man. The money he possessed was sunk in his rubber estate. Lois had no money. Her brother Dick had been beginning life out there when he had died. He had left her nothing. She was entirely dependent on her husband.

Jimmy could not even pay Lois's passage home to England. He could not afford to go back, himself. What then, could he do for the girl he loved and wished to protect?

Lois was ill and tired. Another week with Philip would drive her mad. She must never go back to him. Sanpell refused to let her divorce him, and he could not divorce her because she would never give him the opportunity.

"If I break the vows I made when I married him I shall lose my own self-respect," Lois told Jimmy. "I love you with all my soul, Jimmy, but we mustn't give way to our love."

He reassured her on that point. He loved her far too well to make any demands on her. He was ready to be her friend, to serve her with the utmost loyalty.

They arranged between them, that for the moment Lois should remain here with him; keep the amah to look after her, and see what happened in the future.

Jimmy would see his sister Peggy at the Club that

afternoon, and ask her to come and stay with them.

"If Peggy is with us it will stop tongues wagging in Kuala Lampor," said Jimmy. "While I am away, go and lie down, Lois darling, keep quiet and try not to worry."

Lois did what he wanted. She lay down in the spare room. The amah bathed her temples with eau-de-cologne and fanned her. She was so exhausted that she fell into a deep sleep, in spite of all the worries.

When Jimmy rode back from work, he found Lois on the veranda. The sight of her, so dear, so lovely, thrilled him. He came up the steps of the veranda, wiping his forehead, and smiled at her.

"Lordie, it's hot! Are you baked, Lois?"

"Nearly," she smiled back. "But I had a lovely rest."

"You look better, dear heart."

They sat side by side, facing the straggling, neglected little garden, drinking lime-squash; talking. The conversation quickly turned to Peggy.

"I saw her at the Club and explained things to her," Jimmy said. "She says she'll come along this evening and stay with us for a bit. I'm so relieved, Lois dear; it will make things a little better for you."

Slowly the days dragged by. Lois had a staunch friend in Peggy, but the strain and uncertainty began to tell on her.

"Lois, what can we do," said Jimmy, one morning. "I'm worried about you, darling. If only Philip would set you free."

"We can only wait and hope," said Lois. "Philip may get tired of hanging round. He may give in."

66

"I doubt it," said Jimmy. "I think, if anything, he would like to get at you again."

She shuddered and instinctively leaned nearer Jimmy.

He took her in his arms a moment. He put his brown, tired young face against her soft breast.

"How sick I am of this whole show, Lois! It's knocked all the stuffing out of me. I feel done this morning."

Lois stroked his hair.

"My poor Jimmy. And I've brought all this trouble on you through my rotten marriage."

He tightened his hold of her.

"Don't think for a single moment that I regret anything that has brought you nearer me, my dearest," he said. "Only I want you so, Lois, and I want you to be happy. I want to chuck Malaya and take you home."

She sighed. A tear trickled down her cheek. She wiped it away. She laid the cheek against Jimmy's head.

"Dear, beloved one, don't take it all too badly. One never knows. Something may happen—the tide may soon turn."

He looked up at her. Their lips met and clung in a long kiss, that had more of tenderness in it than passion. Then he said huskily :

"You look so frail, my darling. You aren't feeling ill, are you? You are so precious, Lois. I can't think this hot country is good for you. You look as though you ought to be in England—by the sea."

"Devonshire, for instance, with you," she said wistfully.

"I hate leaving you for an instant," he went on. "I

never feel happy about you unless I'm with you. So many terrible things have happened since we've been out here."

"You've got nerves, my dear," she said. She made an effort to be cheerful for his sake. "Buck up, Jimmy darling. I'm all right. Nothing will happen to me. I've got Peggy to keep me company while you're at work."

He stood up and sighed.

"You're marvellous, Lois, you've got more pluck than all of us put together. Well, I'll be back at half-past twelve. So long, sweetheart."

She waved him out of sight. When his tall figure had vanished, she ceased smiling. She was very heavy-hearted. While Philip existed and denied her her release, how could any of them hope to find happiness?

How long would she and Jimmy, who loved and needed each other so terribly, be able to hold out against their love? And if they gave way to it, how could they hope to be happy? And if they separated for ever, what could there be but unhappiness? It was a wretched, hopeless problem—the whole thing.

At a quarter-past twelve a Malay boy whom Lois recognised as one of her husband's servants, rushed up to her and thrust a scrap of paper into her hand. It read:

"Come to me.—Jimmy."

"Tuanada, come at once!" said the Malay boy excitedly.

Lois let the message fall from her fingers. Her heart began to pound.

"What does it mean?" she asked unsteadily.

"Tuan . . . Tuan Morgan," he said in broken English. "Injured . . . him perhaps dying."

Lois went white to the lips.

"Tuan Morgan—injured—dying—where?" she said.

"Tuan Sanpell's bungalow."

Lois thought she understood. Jimmy had gone to Philip again; maybe to plead for her divorce. They had lost their tempers. Philip, quite possibly, had shot Jimmy in self-defence.

She decided that she would not tell Peggy, who would know about this new disaster soon enough. She just put on her hat and veil, and summoned the amah.

"Come with me, Amah," she said. "To Tuan Sanpell's bungalow."

Outside, Philip's car was waiting. He had sent it for her. Doubtless, as he had shot Jimmy and Jimmy had asked to see her before he died, Philip had been decent enough to grant the request. This was the end then; a bitter, terrible end to all their love and longing.

Lois was like one stunned during the drive to her old home. When the car drew up outside the bungalow, she stepped out and walked up the steps into the living-room like an automaton. She was prepared for any dreadful sight. But she was not prepared to see her husband standing alone in the room, with a sinister smile on his face.

She said :

"Where is Jimmy? Where is he?"

Philip came up to her and seized her wrists.

"How quickly the little bird comes to the whistle of her loving mate!" he sneered.

"Where is Jimmy?" she repeated, shivering from head to foot.

"Just about returning to lunch from his work, I should say," drawled Philip.

The truth struck her then. Jimmy was not here. She had been tricked. She grew cold.

"If Jimmy's not here, why did you send for me, Philip?"

He swung her into his arms and held her like a vice.

"Because I want you. Because I'm not going to allow Morgan to take you away from me. Because I'm not satisfied that I've broken your spirit. It wants a bit more breaking, my Lois. This time you won't be saved by Morgan. The car is waiting outside, and you and your amah are going in it. By the time Mr. Jimmy gets here you'll be gone. And he'll never find you again."

Lois struggled wildly in his arms. Her face was convulsed with fear.

"It's a trap—a trap!" she screamed. "You've tricked me here. Oh, Jimmy—Jim-my!" her voice died away in a long-drawn wail. Philip's lips had fastened on her mouth, stifling her cries. She writhed and moaned as he held her fast, pressing his lips down upon hers, half in passion, half in fiendish malice, the desire to frighten and torture her. Sick and faint she went limp in his embrace.

At last he had lifted his head. He was laughing thickly. She opened her eyes and looked up at him . . . loathing him, terrified of him. His breath smelt strongly of whisky. He had been drinking—even at this hour of the morning. He held her tightly against him; put out a hand and touched her fair, silky hair.

"Dear, sweet little wife," he said. " 'Pon my soul, Lois, there is something irresistible about you. You're so small and delicate and soft. Charming to make love to. You beat all the rest."

70

Her face flushed darkly with hatred and scorn of him.

"Unspeakable cad!" she said, breathing hard. "Oh, you despicable creature, Philip! Let me go—please."

"Not I, Lois, You're coming away with me for a little holiday, right now."

"What do you mean?" she asked, her heart beating so fast with terror that she could scarcely breathe.

"What I say. The car is outside. You and your amah are coming with me to a place where your adored Jimmy won't find you."

"Philip," she said in a low voice of despair. "You can't want to take me away just out of malice. It can't bring you any satisfaction. And Jimmy will look for me. I swear—when I get away from you again—I shall apply for a divorce on the grounds of your disgraceful cruelty."

"Rot!" he said. "By the time I've finished with you, my dear, you'll be doing just what I tell you. Now listen! Are you coming out into the car quietly without any more fuss, or shall I give you something to make you quiet?"

"Philip—for God's sake—"

"Oh, very well," he said grimly. "I'm determined to break you, Lois, and I don't care what lengths I go to. Now, then—"

She screamed as he whipped something out of his pocket; screamed hoarsely again and again.

"Jimmy—oh, save me—Jimmy—Jim-my!"

She felt the sharp prick of a hypodermic needle in her forearm and she knew that she had been doped. A frightful sensation of despair came to her. Her screams died down to moans. She was trapped and done for. Her last thought as she gradually grew stupid and drowsy in her husband's arms, was what poor Jimmy would say when he returned from work to find her gone, and if he would ever succeed in finding her, saving her from this fiend.

Philip looked at his wife. She lay against him limply now. Her eyes were half closed. Without being actually unconscious, Lois was so drugged that she could not resist him or raise her voice in protest against anything he did.

He picked her right up in his arms and carried her out to the waiting car. His handsome face was grimly amused. Lois's amah, patiently standing outside, bowed to him respectfully. He said :

"Get into the car, you. And listen to me. Your mistress is ill. We are going away for a holiday. You will come with us, and keep your ugly mouth closed, d'you see?"

The amah said :

"Yes, yes, Tuan. I will do what you say, Tuan."

She climbed into the car beside the syce. Philip placed Lois's limp little body in the back seat and seated himself beside her.

The syce drove rapidly. The car bumped and swayed over the rough road. They passed occasional bungalows, native villages—harsh, cruel country, baked under the terrible heat of the Malayan sun— poisonous, low-lying swampland infested with fever and rot and disease.

And at last they came to a lonely house off the beaten track, right inland, near a small native village which was built on the Klang river and on the fringe of a dense jungle. This place—by name Trengtan— was known to Philip, although not to many amongst the European population of Kuala Lampor. The girl,

Lalla, who had lived in his bungalow with him before Lois came out to Malaya, had come from Trengtan. Philip had made very handsome presents to Lalla's father, a tribesman of the village; thereby securing his services for evermore.

In addition to this, there was a certain Chinaman named Leng Foo who kept the eating-house on the outskirts of Trengtan, facing the jungle. The men who frequented the place were nearly always of doubtful honesty and bad blood. The women often of easy virtue. There was a tawdriness about the place which was very unpleasant, and it was extremely hot, being close to forest and river, with that damp, pestilent heat which breeds malaria.

Philip would never have brought his wife to such a place had he not lost all sense of proportion. He was drinking heavily; normal reasoning and wisdom were fogged. He had only one evil desire—to break Lois's spirit. In order to do so, he knew he would have to get her to a place like this eating-house on the borders of Trengtan. That she might sicken and die seemed a remote possibility, but he did not honestly care what happened to her, in his temporary madness. The desire to pander to all the evil passions in him swamped every other feeling in the man.

The Chinaman who ran the eating-house knew Philip well by sight and reputation. Sanpell was a rich madman in Leng Foo's opinion: one crazy for drink and women. Leng Foo would do anything for money, and more than once he had helped Philip out of a difficulty. Philip frequented a dancing den in the heart of Singapore which was run by Leng Foo's brother. It was there he had retired after the first row with Jimmy Morgan.

To-day Leng Foo greeted Philip with some surprise as he saw the beautiful English lady lying in Philip's arms. She looked delicate; well-dressed, unlike the usual Malay girl or Eurasian whom men brought to this place.

When Philip explained briefly that the lady was his wife and that she was coming for a "holiday" here with him, Leng Foo was still more surprised. But his bland yellow face expressed nothing. He only smiled and kow-towed to the Englishman, who slipped some money into his hand.

"You are welcome, Mr. Sanpell," he said unctuously. "You may have the house to yourselves. There is nobody here just now."

Philip carried Lois to a big bedroom in the upper part of the bungalow, and laid her on a wide double-bed surrounded by mosquito netting. Sharply he called to the amah to attend to her mistress. The amah, who had discovered a cousin in one of the Chinese boys in Leng Foo's service, hastened to obey. These were strange goings-on for white folk. Never before, in all her years of service, had she known a white lady come to Trengtan, and enter such a house as this. But she was delighted to have found a relative for company and quite pleased to be here. She unpacked the suitcase, which in his own bungalow, Philip had packed with Lois's clothes. She then sat down by the bed with a fan and eau-de-cologne and began to revive Lois, who was just opening her eyes, recovering from the effects of the drug.

An hour later, Lois sat alone in the room, staring out of the window. Her head ached and buzzed. She

74

was white as death. She sat rigid, hands locked in her lap, staring at the strange country which met her gaze — wondering where she had been brought.

She stared round her bedroom. It gave her a feeling of repugnance. It was tawdry and dirty. The atmosphere was incredibly hot, and smelt strongly of joss-sticks. Lois could not bear that smell. Some Chinese must be burning pastilles, downstairs.

When she moved from her cramped position by the window she began to walk up and down the room, holding one slender hand to her aching head. The silence and repression of this horrible bedroom began to get on her nerves. Where was Philip? Where was the amah? She could not bear the loneliness much longer, the sense of horrible strangeness. She felt a thousand miles away from Jimmy.

After awhile Philip came into the room. He looked hot and flushed and cross, as though he had been drinking again. His handsome dark eyes were inflamed.

Lois stumbled to the bed, sank on it and began to cry quietly.

Philip pulled at his collar and tie, took them off, and opened his shirt at the throat.

"It's too damned hot," he muttered.

Lois looked up at him, her face drenched with tears.

"Philip, this is beyond a joke. For God's sake, take me home!"

He gave her a queer look.

"Not I, my dear. Soon as you got back you'd leave me again for Morgan."

"But you don't want me!" she said.

"Oh, yes, I do. You're the only woman I've ever

75

really wanted, body and soul. Don't you like your new surroundings?"

"No, they're horrible. This is a horrible place."

He laughed and thrust his hands into his pockets. He stared at his wife, then round the room, his eyes smouldering.

"Leng Foo's eating-house—a good place for troublesome wives."

"Where are we?" Lois asked.

"Trengtan, dear heart," he said with a mock bow. "A place to which your charming Jimmy will never dream of coming."

Trengtan! The name conveyed nothing to Lois, who knew so little about the Malay States. She only knew that she hated the look of the place; that cruel, oily river; the jungle; the native village. She got up and walked to her husband. She was almost reduced to appealing on her bended knee for mercy—but not quite.

"Philip," she said, trying to speak quietly. "Philip I beg you to take me away from here."

"No," he said.

"But think what people will say if we—vanish like this. And your work—your estate—"

"My estate is in the hands of a competent manager, and I don't care a damn what people say."

"Philip, have you absolutely no decency left?"

"None," he said, his handsome face sneering. "Only the wish to see you beaten."

Anger flamed in her. She straightened herself and flung back her head. Her eyes blazed at him.

"You can kill me, so far as my wretched body is concerned," she said, "but you won't beat me in spirit. I hate and despise you, Philip. You can't touch my mind, my soul, with your beastliness. You can't!"

Her defiance, her pride, maddened Philip. He swung her into his arms. He kissed her savagely until her fair little face and throat were scarlet; burning; until her eyes were pleading for mercy although her lips would not, could not, utter the words.

She fainted, quietly, silently in his arms. . . .

Outside in the shade of a widespread coconut palm, a slim brown Malayan girl with wonderful liquid brown eyes and a full passionate mouth, stood staring up at the window of Lois's bedroom. She could just see the English girl in the arms of the tall, handsome Tuan. She watched half-curiously, half-sullenly; her hands on her hips. There was something very graceful, very panther-like about the girl in her white sarong.

At length she saw Leng Foo, the proprietor of the eating-house, emerge from the bungalow. She slipped behind the big tree, making herself invisible. She watched like a cat. She saw Leng Foo disappear in the direction of the village. She remained concealed behind the tree, watching and waiting for two hours. The figures of the Tuan and his golden-haired Mem were no longer visible.

At sundown the Malay girl was still vigilant. Leng Foo remained in the village. And now the Tuan came out of the rest-house. His white linen suit was immaculate. His hair was well-oiled and brushed. His handsome face, ravaged with evil passions, bore a satisfied smile. He walked so near the coconut palm that the Malay girl could have put out a hand and touched him. But he did not see her. She looked after him, her dark, gleaming eyes half-shut. Her red lips curled back from her splendid teeth. She said something under her breath . . . something passionate and furious in her native tongue. Then quick as thought, she darted forward, entered the eating-house, and stole up to the Tuanada's bed-room unnoticed.

Lois Sanpell was in bed. She was lying on the pillows; eyes closed; small face white and pinched with exhaustion. She had been through a terrible scene with Philip. She was too numbed with pain, both mental and physical, to care much what happened to her now. She only wished to die.

She opened her eyes to see the Malay girl in the white sarong standing by the bed, staring down at her. She sat up at once, alert and startled, all her nerves on edge.

"Who are you? What do you want?" she asked.

"I'm Lalla, Mem," said the girl in tolerable English.

"Lalla?" repeated Lois dully.

"Lalla, who used to be with the Tuan."

Then Lois remembered . . . knew where she had seen this slim, golden-skinned girl. In the garden outside her own bungalow . . . clutching at Philip's arm. And Philip had been beating her cruelly. She remembered what the Malay boy had told her about Lalla. The hot blood dyed her white little face. She sank back on to the pillows.

"Go away," she said.

"Listen, Mem," said the girl. "Lalla no like the Tuan for taking new Mem, and beating Lalla. Lalla want revenge."

Lois looked at the girl with more interest.

"What do you mean?" she whispered.

"Mem no like it here," the girl whispered back. "Lalla help you get away, eh?"

Lois drew a deep breath. To get away from her

78

husband; from his inhuman cruelty; his dark, evil passions, ah . . . if only she could! She pointed to the dressing-table on which lay a jewelled wrist-watch which she had just taken off.

"Look, Lalla," she gasped, "that watch. It is valuable. The diamonds are worth something. Take that. I'll give it to you if you will help me."

The Malay girl picked up the watch and examined it with childish delight.

"For me, Mem?" she said.

"Yes, yes," said Lois. "And more . . . more if you will take a message for me to Tuan Morgan at Kuala Lampor. You know him?"

"Yes, Mem."

"Then go—go at once. Tell him where I am and ask him to save me."

"Very well, Mem," said Lalla. Proudly she put the diamond wristlet watch on her bare brown arm: then listened to its ticking.

Lois's eyes filled with hot tears.

"Oh, go quickly, then, Lalla, or I think I shall die!"

Lalla moved towards the door.

Lois added: "How will you get to Kuala Lampor?"

"I walk. Maybe one day, two day," said Lalla.

"God grant you get there," said Lois in an agony of impatience. "But go now—go quickly and show the Tuan Morgan that watch. He will know for certain then, that you have come from me."

Lalla went out on to the balcony of Lois's room. She peered about her. The day was ending. It was rapidly growing dark. One or two stars blazed in the sky. The tropic night was almost as unbearably hot as the day had been. Like a cat, Lalla swung her slim body over the railings of the balcony and dropped on to the ground below. Then she vanished.

When Philip Sanpell returned to his wife that night, he was so drunk that he could only stumble on to the bed and lie there, fully-dressed, snoring.

Lois lay beside him sleepless and feverish. But her heart beat high with hope, the first hope she had had since she had found herself in Philip's hands. All night long she thought of the Malay girl; prayed that she would reach Jimmy safely, and that Jimmy would come and deliver her from the hands of Philip Sanpell.

The next night, Jimmy Morgan and Peggy, his young sister, sat side by side on the veranda of his bungalow, talking in a state of acute depression.

The last two days, so far as Jimmy was concerned, had been hectic and dreadful. When he had come back to lunch yesterday to be met by a frantic Peggy, informing him that Lois had completely vanished, he had nearly gone mad with anxiety.

Exhaustive inquiries had led to the information that Lois had received a message from one of the Tuan Sanpell's "boys" and had gone with him at midday. Jimmy then knew that Lois had gone to her own home; guessed that she had been tricked by Sanpell.

He immediately rode out to Sanpell's bungalow. But there he met with disappointment and fresh worry. Lois was not there. Philip was not there. Philip's servants were either too afraid of him or too highly paid to give away any information about their master. Neither bribes nor threats from Jimmy produced any result. The Tuan and the Tuanada had gone away. That was all Jimmy could ascertain.

He returned to his own home, to Peggy, completely defeated.

"We only know one thing, Peggy," he said. "Lois went home and she has gone away with Sanpell. But why and where, God alone knows."

At the Club he could extract no further information, no clues as to the whereabouts of the Sanpells. Nobody had seen them.

To-night Jimmy and Peggy reviewed the situation and found themselves just as puzzled as ever and utterly miserable. The bungalow without Lois was terrible. Jimmy was like a lost soul. There was not a smile to be got out of him. Peggy was also genuinely distressed and concerned about Lois who had endeared herself for ever to the younger girl.

"I simply can't understand it, Jimmy," Peggy said to-night. "From all Lois said, I am positive she would never of her own free will, have returned to Philip."

"I'm sure of that too," said Jimmy, his brows drawn together in a deep frown. "Therefore we can take it for granted that Sanpell has tricked her—taken her off against her will."

"Oh, poor, poor little Lois!" wailed Peggy.

"Don't," said Jimmy, his face white and drawn. "I can't bear to think of it. If only I knew where to find her."

Jimmy's thoughts were intolerable. He had a vivid imagination. When he pictured Lois in the hands of Sanpell again it drove him mad. He tried not to think about her. But he was obsessed with the worry and distress of it.

He heard footsteps breaking the silence of the starlit night and looked up. A Malay boy in a white sarong advanced respectfully.

"Tuan, come quickly, please."

"What is it?" asked Jimmy sharply.

"Malay girl close by — her dying, Tuan."

"Dying?" asked Jimmy, rising to his feet. "But why? — what has happened?"

"Don't know, Tuan. But she ask for you."

"Asks for me?" said Jimmy, astonished. He did not for the moment connect any native girl with Lois.

"Yes, Tuan — quickly, please," said the boy.

"I'd better go," said Jimmy to his sister. "Will you come, old thing?"

"Yes, I might as well," said Peggy.

They walked arm in arm through the moonlit garden down the road, following the Malay. Finally they came to a standstill. Huddled on the dusty roadside was the figure of a native girl. Her white sarong was very dirty; her bare feet were torn and bleeding. Her face had that greyish tint which Jimmy recognised at once as a sign of approaching death. He had seen that look on the faces of dying natives before.

He went down on one knee beside her looking at her curiously.

"You want me?" he asked in her own language.

Her eyes slowly opened. They were full of pain. She gasped out a few words.

"Tuan Morgan. I am Lalla. I come many miles and have no food and fever. I dying."

"But why do you want me?" asked Jimmy. The name "Lalla" conveyed nothing to him.

She struggled to speak, but seemed unable to get out the words. She lifted her arm and pointed to it. Something flashed in the moonlight. And then Jimmy saw the diamond wristlet watch . . . the gleam of diamonds

82

on the girl's bare arm. His heart gave a terrific leap and nearly stopped beating. He seized the girl's arm; turned to Peggy.

"Peg—look at this! It's Lois's watch!"

"Lois's watch?" echoed Peggy, her blue eyes round with wonder.

"Yes, I'd know it anywhere." Jimmy bent over the Malay girl, his heart pumping wildly. "Where have you come from? This watch belongs to Tuanada Sanpell. Where is she?"

The girl did not answer. Her eyes were closed. The Malay boy standing beside them, said:

"Maybe she is dead, Tuan."

Jimmy grew frantic.

"Lalla, Lalla, speak," he said in an agony of impatience. "Tell me where the Tuanada is."

Lalla opened her eyes. They were filmed and full of the terror of death. She tried hard to answer Jimmy. Something rattled in her throat. Then her dusky head fell back on his arm.

Jimmy's face went grey in the moonlight. He laid the girl gently down on the road and stood up. He looked at Peggy with eyes of sheer despair.

"Oh, Peg, Peg, she's gone," he said. "And we don't know now where Lois is!"

Peggy began to cry.

"Jimmy, it's horrible. Jimmy, what can we do?"

Jimmy shook his head. He was dumb. He looked down at the still form of the Malaya girl who had come to tell him where to find Lois and had died, tragically, before she could speak the important words.

How still she lay! he thought. Her face was like

polished bronze in the light of the moon; a beautiful carven face, with all terror and suffering wiped out by the fingers of Death who is, after all, the supreme sculptor!

Poor little Malaya girl! Obviously she had suffered. He knew nothing of her; had not known Philip Sanpell in the days when Lalla lived in his bungalow. But he gauged that she had come many difficult miles and had gone through pain and misery to reach him. Her feet were torn and bleeding. She must have had an acute attack of some pestilent fever which had finished her off suddenly, swiftly, like this.

The diamond wristlet-watch still glittered on her wrist. Lois's watch. Jimmy's heart contracted. He stooped down and gently slid the expanding bracelet off the arm which was already growing cold. He shuddered; put his ear to the tiny watch. He could hear it ticking. And perhaps only a few short hours ago it had ticked like that against Lois's wrist. He could scarcely bear it. A lump rose in his throat.

"Oh, Peg," he said huskily. "It's too damnable. Lois must have sent this girl with a message. This watch is certain proof. I know it so well."

"You think she is in some danger?"

"God alone knows, but I feel she sent some urgent message with the girl." Jimmy put a hand to his brow. It was hot and wet. Then he slid Lois's watch into his pocket, and put an arm about his sister. "Come on, old thing. We must go home."

Peggy cast a shuddering look at the rigid body lying on the white, dusty road.

"What about—her?" she whispered.

"The boy must inform the *mata-mata*," said

Jimmy. "I'll give him orders. We can say nothing but that we found her like this."

"We can't possibly trace where she came from?"

"Impossible," said Jimmy. "Only she could have told us, poor girl. But we might make inquiries as to where her home is. I could nose round there and see if anyone knows anything about Lois."

Brother and sister moved off, their arms about each other. Peggy looked at Jimmy and saw tears in his eyes. Tears in Jimmy's eyes! That nearly broke her heart.

"Oh, Jimmy darling," she said, nestling her curly head against his shoulder. "Don't be too cut up. Things will work out all right."

"I love her so, Peg," he said, with an unusual outburst of emotion. "And I'm powerless to go to her. Just because I don't know where she is. It's killing me!"

They walked into the bungalow. Jimmy flung himself into a chair; pulled out a pipe and lit it gloomily. Peggy sat near him, the tears falling silently down her pretty face.

Jimmy leaned over and took her hand. Through the man's mind the most maddening thoughts of Lois chased one after the other. Torturing visions of Lois in danger; in misery; calling for him; expecting him. Poor hapless Lois, relying on the native girl to reach him and give him her message.

"God—my God—why did the girl die?" at length Jimmy broke out, his teeth clenched over the stem of his pipe. "Peg, it's enough to send one insane. Where did she come from?"

"I know, it's frightful," said Peggy with a sob.

"Poor kid, this isn't any too good for you. I think you ought to go back to England."

But Peggy sprang up, flushed and wild-eyed, and refused to go.

"You're not to send me home, Jimmy—you're not to. I couldn't bear it. I can't leave you like this. I can't leave Malaya until I know that Lois is safe and sound with you. You must let me stay and be with you. Don't you want me, Jimmy?"

"I love to have you, old thing," he said kindly. "But it's bad for you—all this excitement and emotion. And it's my battle—I ought to fight it alone."

Peggy flung herself on her knees beside her brother's chair.

"Let me fight it with you. Let me help you find Lois. Oh, please don't send me away!"

Jimmy put a hand on her head, ruffled the brown, crisp hair so like his own. He was moved by her attitude.

"All right, old thing," he said huskily. "Don't worry, I won't send you home if you want to stay with me. It is nice to have you to talk to, I'd go mad if I were alone."

"Lois will come back. I know she will," said Peggy. "Don't despair, darling old Jimmy."

But Jimmy felt very close to despair that night.

In the morning, with the commencement of another fiercely hot day, he took action. He neglected the estate. He rode round furiously, trying to find out something about the dead Malaya girl. By this time the *mata-mata* of the district had the affair in hand. The body of the unfortunate Lalla had been claimed, so Jimmy was told, by an old white-haired Malaya from a place called Trengtan.

"The girl's name was Lalla and she came from Trengtan. The old man is her father. He turned up at dawn. You know, news spreads like wildfire amongst these natives," the British Commissioner of police in Kuala Lampor informed Jimmy. "That boy who found the girl in the roadway last night told his friend and his friend told another, and so on. Every Malaya in the district knows the girl, of course."

Jimmy listened to this with intense interest.

"She comes from Trengtan!" he said excitedly, "that isn't very far from K.L."

"A couple of hours in a car," said the other man. He looked at Jimmy Morgan curiously. "You seem very interested in this girl's death," he added with a smile. "What's up, Morgan?"

Jimmy muttered something unintelligible, and departed. He could not explain to the other man, who was virtually a stranger, that it meant everything in the world to him to find out where the girl, Lalla, had come from.

Everybody in K.L. knew that the Sanpells had mysteriously vanished. But only a handful were aware of Jimmy's particular interest in Lois; and none knew how painfully anxious he was on Lois's behalf. It would only set the tongues of scandal wagging to spread abroad the news that Lois Sanpell's wristwatch had been found on Lalla's arm; that Lois had sent for Jimmy. This was a battle which, unfortunately, he must fight alone, without help from the police. Lois was Sanpell's wife; he had a right to take her away if he wished to. That was the frightful part of it.

But now that Jimmy had a clue to Lois's whereabouts he did not mean to rest until he had followed it up. Lalla came from Trengtan. Lalla's father had trekked from Trengtan at dawn and claimed her body.

Jimmy made up his mind to go to Trengtan.

"Lois may or may not be there," he told Peggy. "It's a chance, but I'll take it. I must see Lalla's father, anyhow."

A man whom Jimmy knew well lent him a two-seater car. He drove to Trengtan early that afternoon.

Peggy begged to be allowed to go with him, but this Jimmy refused.

"Trengtan's a filthy place on the river—full of germs," he said. "I hope to God Lois isn't there, in a way; although I want to find her. But I won't take you, old thing. You stay in the bungalow, and if I don't come back in forty-eight hours send the *mata-mata* after me."

Peggy went white and clung to her brother.

"Jimmy, for heaven's sake take care of yourself. Are you going into danger?"

"I hope not, dear," he said.

"Ought you to go alone? Have you a revolver?"

"Yes, I've got a revolver," he laughed, and kissed her cheek, "Buck up, old lady. I'm not dead yet, and I don't suppose there's the slightest danger in it, unless Sanpell's there, blind drunk, and gets a bullet in me before I get one in him."

He was joking. But Peggy was frantic with anxiety.

"Oh, do take care," were her last words as Jimmy drove off in the car.

Since dawn that morning Lois Sanpell had been awake, feverishly wondering if Lalla had reached

Jimmy's bungalow and delivered her message to him.

It was now long past mid-day. The golden shadows of the fiercely hot day were lengthening. It was so unbearably hot in Lois's bedroom that she could hardly breathe. She felt exhausted. Philip had slept off the effects of too much drink till mid-day. Then he had risen in a foul temper; flung on some clothes and marched out of the eating-house, looking a disgusting, unshaven wreck, very unlike the usual debonair Philip.

Lois shuddered at the thought of him. He had tortured her, just to amuse himself, for a few moments before he left her. Sneered at her; taunted her about Jimmy; sworn at her when she begged him to take her back to Kuala Lampor.

"You'd only fly back to your beloved Jimmy's bungalow. No thanks. I want you with me, and this is the place we'll stay in," he had said roughly.

"But, Philip, we can't stay here for ever. I shall be ill in this horrible place."

"Oh, it takes a lot to kill one off," he had replied brutally. "You can stand it here for a bit; until you know how to treat your husband properly."

"What do you want of me?" she had asked in sheer despair.

"I want to break your spirit," he had retorted viciously. "Make you crawl to me; beg for my love, kiss me of your own accord."

"You think I can do that after all you have done to me?" she had asked in horror.

"Very well—so long as you're so proud and reserved and fastidious—you must pay for it," he had

89

said. "You'll suffer, my dear angel, for every time you shrink away from my kisses."

She thought of him now, in solitude, as a crazy, inhuman creature. No sane man could wish to cause a woman so much suffering as he caused her. He seemed to delight in humiliating her. Her reserve, her pride, her delicacy of tastes—everything seemed to infuriate Philip and rouse the darkest passions in him. She wondered, sometimes, if he would succeed in breaking her? How long would she stand this sort of existence? How long would it be, before she did, virtually, crawl to him; beg him to kiss her, in order to put him in a good humour.

Yet the mere idea revolted her. She loathed him now so utterly that the mere sound of his approaching footsteps outside her bedroom door made her blanch and shiver.

The hours dragged by. Philip did not come back. She supposed he was in the village again, drinking. She put her hands up to her face and felt sick with the thought of him returning to torture her; submit her to all the indignities that seemed to amuse and satisfy him. She kept on thinking of Lalla. Had Lalla reached Jimmy? Had she kept her word? Would Jimmy come?

Her amah waddled into the room.

"Mem have some tea?" she asked.

"Yes," said Lois. She did not even turn her fair little head to look at the amah. She had grown to hate and despise the Chinese woman.

At first she had imagined it possible to bribe her, make her help her to get out of this place. But she soon gave that up. The amah was afraid of Philip; she was a relative of some boy in this rest-house. She was not to be bribed. And Lois felt that in these days there was a hateful touch of contempt behind the amah's oily courtesy—She must, of course, despise white folk who behaved as the Tuan behaved, and the Mem was the Tuan's wife so she must be despised also.

The amah brought her the tea. Lois drank it, but did not touch the biscuits on the tray. They looked dirty—like the tray. Everything in this horrible house was dirty. Lois shrank from eating or drinking anything. But Philip forced her to eat; stood over her while she swallowed her food. He was not going to allow her to get ill through lack of nourishment.

Nevertheless, she felt ill and broken to-day. She sat on the balcony in a pale yellow silk frock. Her face was drawn; her lips pale and pinched. Her eyes were much too large for her small face, and there was an expression of fear and misery in them which would have broken the heart of any human being who loved her.

Lois never once contemplated running away from the eating-house. She took it for granted that it would be a waste of time to try. Even if she escaped the vigilant eyes of the amah or of Leng Foo, she could not possibly get far on foot in this terrific heat. Besides which, she did not know the way. She would soon get lost in such a wild country.

Sometimes she looked at the glittering, oily river and wished she were drowned in it—dead, at peace—finished with all the horror and pain and misery of her present life. But such thoughts were always followed by remorse. She had no right to feel like that, she told herself. No human being had a right to feel suicidal. There was always hope . . . hope of better days . . . purer living. With any luck Lalla would find

Jimmy, and Jimmy would save her. She thought of the man she loved with indescribable yearning. His chivalry, his tenderness, his devotion . . . how terribly she needed them . . . needed him! To her he was the perfect knight in shining armour. And Philip . . . Philip was a devil . . . a monster of iniquity.

The afternoon passed. Darkness fell swiftly. The amah brought the oil lamp up to Lois's bedroom. Lois hated the tawdry, dirty room in the yellow light of the lamp. It cast horrible shadows on the ceiling and walls. It made her frightened and depressed. Her nerves were all to pieces. At times she wanted even Philip to come back. She was afraid of the natives . . . particularly of the smooth-faced, slant-eyed Leng Foo, downstairs—the unprincipled rogue who ran the place.

The amah closed the balcony windows; drew the mosquito netting across, and departed. Lois dragged herself to the bed and sat down limply, her head drooping. It had been a long, terrible day. And Jimmy had not come. She began to believe that Jimmy would never come.

Suddenly she heard a commotion downstairs. She raised her head and listened. She heard men's voices raised; a shout; a revolver shot. Her pinched face grew hot.

She rushed to the door and shook the handle. The amah had orders to lock that door from the outside. It was of course locked now.

Then she heard a man's voice cry her name:

"Lois, Lois!"

She stood like one paralysed, eyes dilated, mouth open. And her heart gave a great jerk. It was not Philip who had called her. *It was Jimmy*. That was

Jimmy's voice. She could not possibly mistake it.

Jimmy was here downstairs. But what was that shot. Who had been shot?

She stood rigid, straining her ears, heart pounding, every drop of blood in her body leaping with the excitement. Now there was dead silence. A silence that terrified her. What had happened, downstairs? Was it Jimmy who had been shot?

Lois suddenly shrieked aloud and beat on the door with her clenched hands.

"Jimmy—Jimmy!" she screamed. She was beside herself with fear.

Then came running footsteps. Somebody unlocked the door. Philip came into the room. She tried to rush past him, still screaming; all her control gone.

"Jimmy—Jimmy's downstairs—*Jimmy!*"

Philip caught her by the arm and swung her back.

"Little fool! Shut up!" he said. "Yes, Jimmy is downstairs. He's the biggest fool. Thought he was going to rescue you from me, eh? Well, he's got what he deserved for interfering between husband and wife."

Lois hung in her husband's grasp, shivering violently. She was trying to stifle her cries, but hysteria was gripping her, and she was like one mad with excitement and fear.

"Where is he? What have you done to him? Oh, you fiend, you fiend! Let me go to Jimmy!" she screamed.

Philip shook her.

"Be quiet," he said. "Be quiet I say!"

She grew suddenly still. She shivered, as though with ague; her teeth chattered. But she ceased screaming. Her great, frightened eyes stared at Philip.

In the yellow gleam of the lamplight he looked demoniacal. Still unshaven and untidy, there were no traces of his usual good looks in his face to-night. He was livid and his eyes were terrible. His lips snarled back from his teeth with a savage laugh.

"You shall see your lover, my dear," he said. "And he shall see you. Come along."

Lois's hysteria had spent itself. She was absolutely quiet now. She said in a low, hoarse little voice :

"Philip, what have you done to Jimmy ?"

"Shot him," said Philip brutally.

Lois's eyelids half closed. She swayed and her husband put an arm about her.

"You have — killed him ?"

"By no means," said Philip. "Only incapacitated him for the moment. He came nosing round Trengtan after you — trying to get information out of Lalla's father. It appears that Lalla died outside Morgan's bungalow last night. And somehow — I don't know why or how — Morgan guessed you were here in Trengtan, and followed. But Lalla's father happens to be in my pay, and he told me Morgan was after you. Morgan came here and demanded to see you — nearly put a bullet through Leng Foo, so I put one through him !"

Lois mustered all her strength. She was near to fainting, but she managed to stave off that sick, dizzy sensation. Her very heart was sick within her. She understood now. Poor Jimmy. Oh, poor Jimmy. He had been shot — because of her.

She set her teeth.

"Take me to Jimmy," she said.

"With pleasure," said Philip with a mock bow. "And then you can pack up and come home. Mr.

Interfering Morgan can remain in Trengtan."

He seized her arm and took her out of the room. He half-led, half-carried her down the wooden stairs. In a big, bare room—a kind of public lounge with small wooden tables and chairs, the walls covered with garish European posters—a little crowd of Chinese were gathered round the form of a man who lay on the floor.

Philip said:

"Get the hell out, all of you. Leng Foo, clear 'em out."

Leng Foo rubbed his hands and bowed. He was feeling amiably disposed towards Mr. Sanpell. The English stranger had threatened him with a revolver and Mr. Sanpell had shot him. Leng Foo did not forget a service. He cleared the room, and Lois, leaning on her husband's arm, saw Jimmy Morgan lying on the bare-boarded floor.

Jimmy was a sorry sight. He had been fighting. His brown curly hair was matted with blood and dust. His eyes were closed. His face was livid and bruised. One arm—where Philip had shot him—was tied up roughly with a piece of roller-towelling.

For a moment Lois's heart seemed to stand still with anguish. Then she rushed forward and knelt beside him. She lifted his head on her lap.

"Jimmy, Jimmy," she said.

He opened his eyes—darkly blue—full of pain. He saw the beloved familiar face bending over him, and the faintest smile lit up his features.

"Lois darling, is it really you?" He stretched up his left arm and put it about her. His head fell against her shoulder. "I'm 'fraid I made a mess of things—they got me, Lois—my arm—I feel so weak."

Lois turned to her husband.

"You can't leave him like this—you devil!" she said passionately. "He'll bleed to death. His arm must be seen to properly—at once."

Philip lounged against the door and lit a cigarette. He smiled at her, a sneering, malicious smile.

"I'm not going to bother about him. It's his own fault if he does bleed to death. By the way I'm enjoying the little scene—touching reunion between my unfaithful wife and her lover."

Lois gave him a look of unspeakable scorn and loathing.

"You know that I have never been unfaithful to you," she said. "Philip, Philip, for God's sake be decent—send for a doctor."

"There are no doctors in Trengtan," said Philip, with a short laugh. "But Leng Foo understands medicine. He shall bind up Mr. Morgan's arm, when I choose to send for him."

Lois turned to Jimmy. He struggled into a sitting position, wincing with the agony of his shattered arm. He had had a tough struggle with Leng Foo before Sanpell had come in and shot him. He felt altogether battered and broken. Loss of blood made him feel stupidly weak.

But the magic of Lois's presence, the touch of her hand, revived him considerably. His brain grew clearer. He saw Philip standing by the door, smiling in his devilish fashion. He saw Lois . . . white, drawn, shadowy-eyed, bending over him. He realised how thin she had grown. What had Sanpell done to her?

"Lois," he said. "My dear, you must get away from this place."

96

"Oh, Jimmy, I want to—I'm nearly dead," she whispered.

Then Philip sprang forward and pulled her brutally away from Jimmy. He crushed her in his arms.

"My wife, thank you," he said. "Not yours, Morgan."

Jimmy set his teeth. He was feeling confoundedly faint again, but he struggled against the mists. He looked up at Sanpell's livid face.

"You're crazy—absolutely crazy," he said. "Take Lois out of this ghastly place—at once."

"I intend to," said Philip, pleasantly. "She will go back to Kuala Lampor with me to-night. But you shall stay here."

Lois struggled in her husband's arms.

"Philip, Philip, let Jimmy go back with us," she said. "I'll stay with you, Philip—I'll do whatever you want—I swear it—only let Jimmy go back with us. Don't leave him in this horrible place."

"Ha, ha!" said Philip. "Almost crawling, aren't you, darling? But I'm afraid I can't humour you over this. Morgan has interfered with me once too often. He can stay here and die."

Lois screamed. Jimmy was trying to drag himself along the floor to her. Their eyes met in fear and agony. Then Philip put out a foot and savagely kicked Jimmy back.

"You've knocked me down and you've taken Lois from me," he said. "Now, it's my turn, Morgan."

Then he picked Lois right up in his arms—such a thin, piteous little figure in the yellow frock—looking over his shoulder at Jimmy and laughing mockingly.

"Ta-ta, Morgan. Enjoy your holiday with Leng Foo. He understands torture better than I do, being a

Chinaman. Lois and I will be very happy together in future."

The door slammed after him. Jimmy heard Lois crying. And then he fainted dead away.

CHAPTER IV

WHEN Jimmy Morgan opened his eyes again, he was lying on the bed in the room which Lois had recently occupied. His arms were pinioned to his sides. His feet were tied together. He could not move. But he looked dazedly around him, became conscious that it was still night-time.

His head was splitting with pain. His whole body felt sore as though he had been kicked and bruised. His arm was still wrapped round with the blood-stained towel.

The mists cleared slowly in his brain. Then he began to think—to remember. His last vision of Lois, poor little Lois, had been in her husband's arms. She had been carried away—heaven knew where—by that brute Sanpell.

"Where have you been taken? What are they doing to you, Lois, my little love?" he thought.

The deadly gravity of his own position struck Jimmy more acutely as he lay there, while the moments dragged by, reviewing the situation. Peggy, his little sister would be anxious. Ah! A most consoling thought struck him now. He had warned Peggy to send the police for him if he failed to return home. Peggy, alone, knew that he had come to Lalla's home in search of Lois.

Jimmy smiled grimly in the darkness.

He was not as lost as he had first thought.

But he had Leng Foo to reckon with yet. He had been lying there cramped and tortured with thirst in the stifling heat of the bedroom for some hours, when the door opened and Leng Foo entered, a revolver in one hand, an oil lamp in the other. The tawdry bed-room was flooded with the yellow light. It showed the Chinaman's face, flat, bland, evil, beady eyes fixed upon the Englishman. Jimmy looked up at him.

"Leng Foo," he said, "you'll be well advised to let me go—and at once."

Leng Foo smiled.

"I regret," he said, "Velly impossible."

"It will be made 'velly impossible' for you, you yellow swine, when I get back to Kuala Lampor," said Jimmy savagely. "You'll get hard labour for this sort of game, my friend."

Leng Foo's black eyes became slits.

"Mr. Morgan will not get back to Kuala Lampor, maybe," he said in an oily voice. "Leng Foo no damn fool."

Jimmy tried to keep his temper. He realised that it would be folly to quarrel with the man who was his gaoler. He said, more quietly :

"Look here, Leng Foo, get me a drink, and let's talk this over. If it's a question of money—I've got a bit."

Leng Foo set the lamp on the dressing-table, then came to the foot of the bed and leaned over it. He smiled again, evilly.

"Leng Foo plenty rich man. No want money. But keep fliends with Mr. Sanpell, who save Leng Foo's life. You would velly much have killed Leng Foo."

Jimmy digested this in silence. He cursed under his breath. What had induced him to spring at the China-man when he arrived ? It had been fatal.

"Leng Foo," he said after a pause. "If you let me go now, I'll give you a written guarantee that you won't be touched for what you have done to-night. But if you keep me here my friends will find out where I am, and you will be sentenced for it."

The Chinaman gave a low chuckle. His bland countenance expressed supreme contempt.

"Leng Foo think that of British police. No find Mr. Morgan in Leng Foo's eating-house. Leng Foo no damn fool. You come along me right away now."

Jimmy struggled with the rope that bound his hands and feet, but it was futile. He was firmly tied and the effort only hurt him. He looked up at the Chinaman with bloodshot eyes.

"Be careful, Leng Foo," he warned him. "If you do me in you'll swing for it. I swear you will. The British police are not such fools as you think. They'll trace me here and they'll get you for it."

Leng Foo spat on the floor again.

"Bah," he said, "get up."

Jimmy staggered on to his feet and rocked there. The pain in his arms and his head made him feel sick and dizzy.

"God, if I had my hands free," he thought. "If I could fight for it. But I haven't a dog's chance like this."

"Where are you taking me?" he asked. "Or are you going to finish me off now?"

"No finish you off," said Leng Foo sweetly. "Leng Foo no commit murder. Mr. Morgan maybe died natural death. . . . fever, loss of blood. Leng Foo has been asked by Mr. Sanpell to take care of Mr. Morgan."

"I see," said Jimmy between his teeth. "Slow death from natural causes, eh?"

He felt deadly sick . . . that feeling of nausea which

accompanies extremity of fear. Jimmy would never have admitted it, never have crawled to Leng Foo's feet for mercy, but he was afraid. He was a very human, natural person; he was young and strong and ardent; he was full of the joy of life; he adored Lois. He did not want to die—at least not a dog's death in the hands of this yellow beast.

Leng Foo said very softly:

"I wish you good-bye, and velly pleasant journey Mr. Morgan."

"The same to you," said Jimmy thickly. "I'd like to shake hands. You wouldn't care to untie the rope I suppose?"

The Chinaman shouted something in his own language. Two dark-skinned boys in blue cotton suits came up the stairs. Leng Foo gave them an order. They grinned, and the next instant Jimmy was lifted between the pair of them and carried downstairs. Leng Foo followed with his lamp and revolver.

He was put into a litter on two poles, carried by the boys and taken rapidly through the darkness to the edge of the river. He was then placed in a boat. He heard the lap-lap of the water against the boat's sides. Sick at heart and half insensible with pain and thirst, Jimmy felt himself being rowed swiftly down the river—farther and farther away from civilization and any hope of rescue from his own people.

Lois's feelings, when Philip carried her away from the room in which Jimmy was lying, bordered on madness. But Philip's arms held her tightly and his voice rough and hoarse against her ear, told her repeatedly to "shut up".

"You won't gain anything by this howling. So stop it, Lois," he kept on snarling at her. "It's your own fault if you don't like what's happened."

Lois beat with her small, hot hands against his face. "Let me go back—take me back to him. Jimmy! Jimmy!" Her voice died away in a long wailing cry. She lay rigid in Philip's arms. She was in a state of extreme mental exhaustion and this was more than she could bear. She drifted into unconsciousness.

It was a prolonged faint for Lois, punctuated by terrible nightmares, during which she half-woke, moaning; sobbing. But she knew nothing of the long drive in the car back to her home in Kuala Lampor.

All that night she was very seriously ill—raving, moaning in delirium. There was no one to look after her but Philip and the boys. The amah was no longer in attendance. Philip had decided that it was wiser to leave the old woman in Leng Foo's house in case she came back here and chatted too freely.

Lois's life now hung in the balance. She was so bad that even Philip began to be afraid. He did not love her. He did not love anybody but himself. But he did not want to lose her, to let her slip like this through his fingers. He did not mean to let death cheat him of his prey.

He sent a boy for a doctor. Not Saunders, the cheery, fair-haired Englishman who attended most of the self-respecting British folk in K.L., but a certain Eurasian named Gruyler, who had recently set up a practice, a somewhat nefarious one, although he was supposed to be a brilliant physician.

Nobody knew who or what he was. The British public did not care. They neither received him in their social circle nor dreamed of having him as their medical adviser. He mainly attended half-castes, natives, and, occasionally the worst kind of European in the Straits.

Philip dared not let Saunders come into his bungalow. He wanted no prying eyes in his affairs at the moment. Gruyler was the fellow for him. So Dr. Gruyler arrived at four that fateful morning. He came into the bungalow, rubbing his hands together and bowing to the ground. He was highly delighted to be called in to Mr. Sanpell's bungalow, to attend to an Englishwoman.

Philip had been drinking heavily, but Lois's serious condition had sobered him now. He had taken a bath and shaved and put on clean, white clothes before Gruyler came. All the doctor saw was a rather haggard, handsome man with inflamed eyes, who might be suffering from funk and nothing else.

"Your wife is veree ill?" Gruyler asked in the clipped careful English, which gave away his mixed blood. He had the thin, dark fingers of a native. Evil hands.

"Damned ill," muttered Philip. "And you've got to pull her through."

Gruyler bowed.

"I'll do my utmost," he said.

Gruyler was a man without principles, but he was a fine physician. Before he had been in Lois's bedroom half an hour he had her case well in hand and was working, coat off, and shirt sleeves rolled up—working feverishly—to save her life.

She lay in the big bed looking like a beautiful, waxen figure; her small, pinched face colourless; her eyes closed; her breath coming very faintly and irregularly. She had passed from a stage of violent delirium to one of extreme exhaustion. Her vitality was at a low ebb. Philip slunk about the room watching, furtively.

"Well?" he rapped out, when at length Gruyler turned from Lois whose wrist he had been holding.

"She is veree weak," he said. "But she will live."

"You're certain?" said Philip hoarsely.

"I hope so," said Gruyler. "Has she received any great shock? Her condition suggests shock—as well as fever."

Philip lowered his gaze.

"Yes, maybe she has," he muttered.

"She has asked several times for a man called 'Jimee'," said the Eurasian smoothly. "And keeps saying he must be saved. I—er—"

"She's raving," Philip broke in. He came up to Gruyler and glared down at the little man. "Raving, do you understand?" he added in a significant tone. "Not all there. Mental case. D'you understand?"

Gruyler's small eyes behind gold-rimmed glasses stared up at the Englishman . . . then blinked once or twice. He smiled and shrugged his shoulders. He understood. There was something funny here . . . very funny. But it was not for him, Maurice Gruyler, to interfere, or kill his own goose in this household. His queer eyes narrowed. He said very softly:

"The poor ladee. Yes, her brain is slightly turned with fever and shock. It is a mental case. One takes no notice of what patients say in these cases."

Philip drew a deep breath. His eyes glittered.

"Splendid!" he said. "And what are your charges?"

Gruyler put a finger to his lips.

"Always a little dearer for mental cases," he said in a silky voice. "Shall we say, one hundred pounds?"

"A cool hundred, eh?" Philip laughed savagely. That was the Eurasian's price for discretion—for treating Lois's case as "mental" and paying no heed to her raving about Jimmy. He dared not refuse to pay it. "All right," he said. "I'll give you a cheque."

Gruyler looked at Lois. Her eyes had opened. She was saying something. He moved to her side.

"Yes?" he said.

She looked up at him. She felt that she was wandering in a maze. The Eurasian had brought down the fever. He had given her miraculous draughts. She was not going to die; but she felt indescribably weak and ill. The thought of Jimmy obsessed her.

"Where am I?" she whispered.

"At home, with your husband," said Gruyler.

She stared up at him with wide, frightened eyes.

"Who are you?"

"Dr. Gruyler, at your service. You have been ill."

"You are a doctor? Oh, then, for God's sake send help to Jimmy—Mr. Morgan—he's in Leng Foo's rest-house in Trengtan—send help—save him—please, doctor—" Her voice rose—two hectic spots flushed her white cheeks. She clutched at the man's arm. In her present condition she did not realise that the man was a Eurasian. She had never heard the name before.

Gruyler laid her gently back on the pillow.

"There, there, all right—you're all right," he said. "Just dreaming. Go to sleep."

"I'm not dreaming," said Lois panting. "Doctor, for God's sake—Jimmy—Leng Foo's house—"

"There, there," he broke in, with maddening indifference to her words. "Go to sleep."

She looked wildly round the room. She saw her husband standing by the window, watching. He looked down at her with a smile on his handsome face. Then he came forward and deliberately bent over and kissed her hot forehead.

"I'm so thankful you're better, darling," he said. "You're only dreaming, as Dr. Gruyler says. Go to sleep now."

A frenzy seized Lois. She began to cry convulsively.

"You must save Jimmy—oh, my God—Philip—you fiend—*you murderer*—"

She broke off. Her voice slurred away. Her eyes closed. A drug that Gruyler had given her had taken effect. She slept. But the ugly word *"murderer"* seemed to linger in the air—repeat itself in the ears of the two men who had heard it. They exchanged glances. Philip went scarlet and looked away. Gruyler smiled. Then he came close to Philip and rubbed his hands together.

"It's going to be a very nastee case, Mr. Sanpell," he said in a tone that suggested compassion. "I'm afraid my fee will be—five hundred pounds."

Philip's head shot up. The muscles of his cheeks worked.

"No, by God—" he began.

"Veree well. I must resign the case—to—say Dr. Saunders," said Gruyler regretfully.

Philip pulled a handkerchief from his pocket, and mopped his forehead. It was wet. He glanced at the piteous, fragile figure of Lois in the bed. Then he clenched his teeth.

"All right. I'll pay," he said.

He wrote out the cheque and handed it to the Eurasian doctor. Gruyler departed, after taking a drink with Philip in a most friendly fashion. He would come again later in the day, he said. And a trained nurse would be necessary. Philip was worried about that, but Gruyler assured him that he knew a girl in Kuala Lampor, who would work for him and hold her tongue.

"She and I have done some—what shall we say—veree difficult cases together," Gruyler told Philip. "She will accept this mental case for me."

"And nobody is to be allowed to see Mrs. Sanpell. Nobody! D'you hear?" Philip said hoarsely. "When she is strong enough to travel, I shall take her to Singapore."

"Quite so," said Gruyler softly. "And until then doctor and nurse will see that nobodee visits Mrs. Sanpell. She must be veree quiet."

After he had driven away, Philip shut the door and returned to Lois's bedside. He stood looking down at her; at the ravaged little face in its frame of silky, blonde hair. Yet he felt no pity for her—only passion —the unceasing mania to take and break her. He would see that Mr. Jimmy Morgan could not interfere with him this time, he told himself savagely.

"You're in my hands now, utterly, Lois," he muttered. "You're my wife, and if I choose to have a half-caste doctor and his nurse for you . . . nobody can interfere with me—"

For several days Lois lay like one half dead in that big, sunlit bedroom; too weak to move even her hands. Everything had to be done for her. Any attempt on her part to get into a sitting posture or any violent talking, made her faint dead away. She could only speak in a whisper. But she was on the road to recovery. Gruyler was a marvellous physician, without a doubt. He had saved her life.

But Lois had grown to loathe Gruyler. She realised, also, that he was siding with Philip. He took no notice of her continual appeals to him to send help to Jimmy.

She did not know what had happened to Jimmy. She thought of him with despair. Probably he was dead by this time. She asked repeatedly for Peggy Morgan, but, of course, no notice was taken of the request. And she did not know that the morning after she had been brought home, Peggy had heard that the Sanpells were back, and had called here and been sent away with the news that Lois was "seriously ill" and that the doctor refused to allow her to see anybody.

Peggy, of course, had left the bungalow in a state of complete bewilderment. Lois was home. Where, then, was Jimmy? And when, after forty-eight hours anxious waiting, Jimmy did not return, Peggy went to her old friends, the Williams's, and put the case in their hands.

Tiny Williams thought it all very queer. Jimmy had told his sister that he was going to Trengtan to find Mrs. Sanpell and Mrs. Sanpell was at home with her husband. What did it mean? He saw that Peggy was in a great state of panic, and fear for her brother. He promised to make investigations.

And while all this was going on, Lois lay helpless, unable to move or act. Gruyler was treating her as if she were off her head and she wondered how long it would be before she really did go off her head. It drove her insane to think of Jimmy in Leng Foo's hands— Jimmy tortured—dying—perhaps dead. . . .

Her one hope of help lay in her hospital nurse. This woman was quite young; thirty-one or two, and handsome in her fashion, with a white skin and reddish hair. She wore a pale grey uniform which suited her. Her name was Monica King. She was a widow, and of English birth and breeding.

Six years ago she had married a Eurasian and had been boycotted by her friends; particularly in Penang where she had received her hospital training. Then her husband had died and she had had to return to nursing. She found no English doctor to give her work. But Gruyler, when he came across her, discovered just what he wanted in Monica King. She was very fond of pretty clothes and extremely vain. She would do anything for money. She nursed all his most shady cases. He had put her on to Lois's case, relying on her tact and discretion.

After years of leading a life which was never quite straight, Monica King had grown hard and unprincipled. Only at very rare intervals did she look back and regret . . . loathe her present life — think of the old, happier days amongst her own people. Such remorse did not last for long. The mercenary side was uppermost. With Dr. Gruyler's help she was saving up quite a nice little sum of money.

Lois disliked Nurse King from the beginning. She treated her as Dr. Gruyler treated her — as a mental patient. It brought Lois to the verge of real madness. Again and again she besought Monica King to send help to Jimmy Morgan. But the woman only smiled at her in a maddening fashion and told her to "keep quiet".

Then, as the days went by, and Nurse King continued with her duties under Dr. Gruyler's eye, she began to feel vaguely sorry for Mrs. Sanpell.

One evening, she bent over the younger girl and said tersely :

"Oh, don't stare at me with those great eyes like that. What is it you want?"

Lois's cheeks flushed crimson. Her weak fingers clutched the nurse's arm.

"I want a message sent to Miss Morgan—you know who I mean—on the neighbouring estate—tell her that her brother is in Leng Foo's house; and to send help at once to him. Oh, Nurse, Nurse, *Nurse*; do it— please! Don't tell the doctor or my husband. Neither of them need know."

"All right," muttered Nurse King. "I'll see Miss Morgan when I go out to-morrow."

Outside the door Monica King came face to face with Philip Sanpell. One look at his face and she knew that he had been listening at the keyhole. She went scarlet. But Philip only smiled very gently and put an arm through hers.

"I want a little talk with you," he said.

"Well?" she said sullenly.

He led her into the living-room and pushed her on to the divan. He sat down beside her, regarding her gravely with his brilliant eyes. He smiled.

"I heard you tell my wife that you would take a message for her to Miss Morgan," he said. "Of course you were only humouring her. You won't do it."

"I'm not so sure," the woman muttered. "I'm getting worried about this case. What's happened to Mr. Morgan? Everybody's talking about him in Kuala Lampor—his strange disappearance . . ."

Philip's eyes narrowed.

"Indeed," he said gently. "Well, why should you worry your head over it? By the way you've got a lovely head. Do you know I adore red hair—Monica?"

His caressing voice, his sudden use of her Christian name, made the woman flush and thrill. All thoughts of the suffering, tormented little creature upstairs, vanished. She turned and looked coquettishly up at the man beside her.

"Naughty!" she murmured. "You shouldn't—!"

He slid a hand over hers.

"Monica," he said huskily. He was a born lover and acted his part to perfection now. "Monica, don't you realise that ever since you came here to nurse Lois, I've been crazy about you? Your wonderful white skin—your flaming hair—"

She shivered with delight. He was so handsome; such a marvellous creature to look at, with his Greek head; his dark luminous eyes and wonderful curved mouth. And who could resist Philip when he chose to be charming? Who, save those who knew the devil behind the mask?

Monica King was a flirt. She was also a woman.

When he took her in a passionate embrace she yielded and clung to him—kissed him back. He was playing a definite game—for his own ends—but apart from it he was always ready to be the lover to a good-looking girl. He whispered against her ear:

"And now, Monica mine, you're not going to repeat anything my poor, mad wife says—to anybody—are you?"

Monica King did not answer for a moment. She seemed dazed, speechless.

She had not dreamed that Philip was attracted by her. Up till now he had not shown her any particular attention. He had appeared to be his wife's lover.

"Adorable Monica," he said. "Your wonderful hair

is flame-colour—like my heart—on fire—with love."

Each word was punctuated with a long kiss. Monica's red head fell back against his shoulder. She shut her eyes; panting, trembling. Then she spoke at last:

"Don't kiss me again," she said, breathing very fast.

"Oh, but please, Monica—"

"No—no," she broke in, "You're driving me mad."

"But I want to. I'm mad myself. You're devilishly attractive, Monica, darling."

"Do you mean that?" she spoke almost piteously. She put up a hand and stroked back his thick dark hair, looked yearningly at his face—a perfect face. How handsome he was! She had never seen more perfect features.

"Oh, Philip," she whispered. "Do you really love me?"

"Yes," he said. "I do."

He touched her starched grey linen nursing frock; her white collar and cuffs. He smiled. "But I hate all this uniform. I want to see you in something soft and feminine. I'd like you in black—black, transparent chiffon. You have a skin like snow. You'd look wonderful in black chiffon with that flaming head of yours."

She shivered with delight. Was there ever such a lover? He knew exactly what to say to please her.

"I shall get a black chiffon dress to-morrow," she said, with an excited little laugh.

"Good," he murmured. "And you shall wear it for me and I shall kiss your throat and your arms, my Monica, and you shall let me brush your hair into flaming glory all over your head."

He caught her close to him again and put his lips against her head. He gave a sigh.

"You've got something lovely on your hair, darling. You don't smell of beastly disinfectants like one would expect a hospital nurse to do. What scent do you use?"

"It's French," Monica King said, with a coquettish look up at him. Her foolish heart beat to suffocation. "It's called '*Adieu sagesse!*' "

Her French accent was atrocious but Philip let it pass.

"That means 'good-bye wisdom'," he whispered.

This philandering with Lois's nurse was really becoming quite an agreeable pastime, he reflected. He had originated the affair for the sake of his own personal safety. He knew it was essential that he should get this woman entirely under his thumb. But he was now beginning to enjoy the game.

Trembling with delight, Monica surrendered to his love-making. Neither of them seemed to remember the girl upstairs, the weak, white, helpless girl who was praying desperately that Monica King would take the message about Jimmy to Peggy Morgan.

After a few moments Philip was more than confident that Monica would never betray him. He returned to the subject of Lois.

"Listen, darling," he said. "My unfortunate wife upstairs is quite insane, you understand—gone here." He touched his forehead significantly. "She's got it into her head that Jimmy Morgan, this friend of hers, has been left to die in Trengtan. Of course, there isn't a grain of truth in it, but if the news is spread round K.L. it might cause a sensation, and people would be pouring in here to make inquiries. This fellow Morgan is missing. Lord knows where he is. He was a friend of Lois's and since her brain has gone she has imagined all these frightful things about him. Just humour her, d'you see?"

"I'll do exactly what you tell me, Philip," Monica said.

"Well, she asked you to tell Miss Morgan various things. You must forget it. And on no account is anyone to visit Lois. Gruyler knows that, and you can keep people away too. I don't want the poor little thing worried. As soon as she can be moved, she must be taken to a private asylum."

"It's terrible for her, but it's worse for you," said Monica. "Fancy a man like you being tied up to a wife who is mental."

"Yes. I have suffered badly," said Philip with a hypocritical sigh. "You can imagine how badly I need your love, your sympathy, your support, Monica darling."

She clung to him passionately.

"You shall have it! Oh, Philip, you've made me divinely happy, and I'll do any mortal thing to comfort you. No worries shall come to you through me."

Half an hour later she put on cap and apron and returned to her patient's bedroom. She was very hot and flushed and her eyes were unnaturally bright, but Lois did not notice these things. She only looked at the nurse with eyes full of intense anxiety.

"Have you seen Miss Morgan? Have you told her?" she asked in her weak voice.

"There, there, don't worry," said Nurse King without meeting her gaze. "I've told her."

Lois's eyes filled with scalding tears. She gave a sob of relief.

"You have? Oh, God bless you, Nurse!"

Monica busied herself about the room. She hid her face from Lois. Her heart was throbbing rather guiltily. She little deserved that fervent blessing from Lois. But she tried to salve her conscience by recalling Philip's words. Lois Sanpell was insane. One need not pay any attention to what she said. Poor Philip! To be landed with a mad wife. Monica's pulses leaped at the memory of Philip's long kisses. She forgot all about her conscience.

Lois, who had no reason to doubt Monica King's statement, shut her eyes and tried to console herself with the belief that now that Peggy knew where Jimmy was to be found, he would be rescued and brought back to her. She was still so weak that she could only lie there, helpless, the tears trickling down her cheeks. She whispered Jimmy's name again and again.

"Oh, my darling, God grant that they get to you in time," was the cry of her heart.

She knew nothing about the fate of two visitors who called to see her that afternoon. Monica King interviewed them. They were Miss Peggy Morgan and Mr. Williams; Jimmy's sister, and his best friend.

Williams was determined to see Lois. Peggy had told him a good many things which had made him suspicious. Peggy, on her part, was longing to question poor Lois and ascertain whether she had seen anything of Jimmy.

Monica King met the occasion, however, with an aplomb and quiet determination, which would have won her many kisses from Philip had he been there to witness it. She definitely refused to allow either Miss Morgan or Mr. Williams into Mrs. Sanpell's bedroom.

"My patient is extremely ill, and must be kept absolutely quiet. Those are the doctor's orders," she said.

Peggy and Tiny Williams exchanged glances. The man's sunbrowned face was perplexed and troubled.

"Damned if I know why Sanpell is having this doctor instead of our own M.O.," he muttered. "It's a very queer affair altogether."

Peggy made another appeal.

"Nurse, it's most important," she said. "I can't quite explain, but it really is essential that I should speak to Lois for a moment."

"More essential than saving her life?" Nurse King's brows went up in well simulated surprise.

"It isn't that surely," said Peggy flushing. "She can't be so frightfully ill."

"Miss Morgan, if you doubt my word, perhaps you will see Dr. Gruyler and ask him," said Monica frigidly.

Peggy bit her lip. She felt helpless; beaten. Yet she lingered. She felt she must see Lois.

"Nurse," she made a last appeal. "Won't you even ask her a question for me, and let me have the answer?"

"Yes, if you wish," said Monica unwillingly.

"Then ask her whether she knows where my brother, Jimmy Morgan, can be found," asked Peggy eagerly.

Monica put her tongue in her cheek and smiled. She told Peggy to wait. She went away. Needless to say she went nowhere near her patient. She returned to Peggy Morgan.

"Mrs. Sanpell sends you her best love. She is quite cross at not being allowed to see you, but she knows it is for her own good. She says she has not seen Mr. Morgan since the day she left his bungalow to return here. Now, I must return to duty, so pardon me if I leave you. Good-afternoon."

Peggy and Tiny were forced to retreat and Nurse King shut the door of the bungalow in their faces. They walked slowly away. Peggy glanced back at the bungalow once or twice.

"It all worries me to death," she said, her eyes full of tears. "Jimmy's disappearance; Lois's mysterious return and illness; that Gruyler man being called in; it's all so queer."

"On the other hand, Jimmy's disappearance may have nothing whatever to do with the Sanpells," said Williams.

"Oh, shall we ever see him again?" asked Peggy, her voice breaking.

"Cheer up, little girl," said Williams. "I'm sure we shall. I shall go along to Trengtan to-morrow and investigate, anyhow."

The day came when Lois could no longer be kept in her room, and she was allowed to come downstairs. She was scarcely able to walk without leaning on the nurse's arm. Philip was at home that day. When Lois tottered into the sitting-room with Monica, he gave her one swift, shamed look, then stared at the floor. If ever conscience assailed him it was at that moment. She looked absolutely broken. There was a tortured expression in her golden eyes that would have melted any heart.

When Monica left them alone, he said :

"Come here, Lois," and held out his hand. But she

still had some spirit left in her. She flushed and put up her own hand as though to ward him off.

"Don't touch me, Philip. I swear if you touch me again I shall kill myself."

"Oh, all right," he mumbled. "Don't worry. I won't. I was only going to say if you'd like to go away—to the sea or something—I'll take you."

"No, thank you," she said.

She sat down on the divan, her thin little hands clasped in her lap, her fair head drooping. Philip scowled at her.

"It's no good you going on fretting about Morgan," he muttered. "I don't suppose he's alive."

She shuddered and hid her face in her hands.

"No, I don't suppose he is now. If he had been alive, he would have come to me. You've murdered him. You're a murderer! You know it."

Philip's handsome face went livid for a moment, then he gave a short laugh.

"Oh, rubbish! Is that the tale you mean to spread around as soon as you can?"

"I shall have no compunction whatsoever in accusing you," she said, suddenly flinging back her head. "You have murdered him—my best friend." Her voice broke, "—and you deserve to pay for it."

He sprang to his feet and suddenly came over to her. His face was working. He was scarlet to the roots of his hair.

"You can't," he said. "You can't accuse me. I tell you, you can't."

"Why not?"

"Because if you do you'll be accusing the father of your child, and that will be a nice thing for the kid, won't it?"

A look of astonishment and horror crossed Lois's white face. Silence for a moment, then she gasped:

"What do you mean? What are you saying?"

"The truth," he said. "Dr. Gruyler and Nurse King told me last night. You don't realise it yourself, but you're going to have a baby. I didn't want it, and I'm sure you didn't, but there it is."

She put her hands to her head. Her heart beat so fast it nearly choked her. But as she sat there thinking, staring before her, she was conscious that Philip was not lying to her this time. The conviction seized her that it was true. She was going to be a mother — the mother of Philip's child. What a ghastly thing....

She hid her face in her hands.

"Once I would have been glad," she said in a low, dreary voice. "Once I would have loved it . . . a little baby of my own. But now . . . how little I want it!"

Suddenly Monica King burst into the room. She looked flushed and flurried.

"What am I to do?" she said hysterically. "There is a man outside who says he's a Mr. Jimmy Morgan, and he must see Mrs. Sanpell at once."

"Morgan!" said Philip blankly, "Morgan...."

"Jimmy!" whispered Lois, her white face, small and pinched, but the golden eyes became suddenly like stars. She staggered on to her feet and rushed to the door, crying his name. "Jimmy — Jimmy — Jimmy!"

And half-way across the room she was met by him . . . the man she had believed dead. She saw him, a pale, thin Jimmy, with his arm in a sling — Jimmy, wearing a filthy, tattered suit . . . but it was Jimmy and not his ghost. The next minute she was clinging to him, sobbing convulsively.

"Jimmy," Lois panted his name, holding him tightly, her thin face glowing. "Jimmy—oh, Jimmy!"

Jimmy Morgan held her close with one arm. Just for an instant these two who loved each other so passionately and who thought they would never see each other again, clung in wordless rapture, oblivious of the world. It was as though Philip Sanpell and Monica King, staring from the doorway, did not exist. They had eyes only for each other. Locked in a wild embrace they stood there . . . he strained her closer until it seemed that Lois's strength—such feeble strength these days . . . gave out. She fell against him; her small fair head sagging. He stared anxiously down at her face. Her eyes were shut. Black lashes curved piteously on the pale cheeks.

"Lois," he said hoarsely. "Lois—open your eyes—look at me—speak to me, darling."

Monica King gave a hysterical laugh.

"Well, I'm blowed," she began, looking across the room at Sanpell. But he cut in sharply.

"Shut up, Monica. Go out. Leave this to me."

Nurse King put her hands on her hips, and tossed her red head insolently.

"You needn't speak to me like that, Phil—" she began again.

He marched across the room, put a hand on her shoulder and pushed her out.

"Oh, go to blazes!" he said violently; shut the door upon her and stood with his back to it. With eyes glittering, half with fear, half with rage, he looked at the man whom he had paid Leng Foo to murder, and wondered how and why Jimmy Morgan was here, alive to-day.

Jimmy had helped Lois to the sofa. Still oblivious of

Philip, ignoring his presence, he knelt beside the woman he adored; chafed her small cold hands; begged her to open her eyes.

The big, golden eyes slowly opened. Lois returned to consciousness. And now she saw the dear, familiar face of Jimmy bending over her. She gave a cry and stretched out her arms to him.

"Then it is you. I haven't been dreaming. Jimmy, Jimmy, take me away—hold me—never let me go again."

"My darling," he said huskily. He laid his head against her breast. He was tired and spent. He had seen hell these last few weeks; a hell from which he had never expected to escape. But here on his knees beside Lois, her soft breast a resting-place for his weary head, it was like heaven. He gave a great sigh. "Darling, darling Lois," he said.

She struggled into a sitting position; raised his head between her hands and looked into his eyes. How blood-shot and darkly blue they seemed, in a face grown pitifully thin. There were dark hollows under those eyes. His frame was worn to the point of emaciation; his clothes were dirty and threadbare. But it was still Jimmy, and to Lois, the dearest face in the world. She began to cry, tears rolling down her cheeks.

"Jimmy, what have they done to you? You look—terrible—"

"Do I?" he laughed shortly. "I'm afraid I'm not fit for your presence really, darling. But I had to come . . . I was crazy with anxiety about you—I came straight here when I got to Kuala Lampor."

Lois opened her eyes as though about to speak, then closed them again. Over Jimmy's shoulder she suddenly caught sight of her husband. With a shock she realised that he had been there all the time. She had been blind, deaf, dumb, with the overwhelming joy of reunion with Jimmy. But now, as she saw Philip's white, furious face, she relapsed into the old state of fear and misery. Jimmy felt her trembling and saw the look in her eyes. He turned his head sharply, and he too became conscious of Sanpell's presence. He drew in a breath, released Lois, and stood up.

"When you've done with my wife, Morgan," Philip said with an unpleasant smile.

"Sanpell," said Jimmy quietly. "I advise you very strongly to keep your tongue between your teeth. You've done quite enough. You may be Lois's husband by law, but that's as far as it goes. When I leave this bungalow, she leaves with me, and we are going straight to the police."

Philip remained standing by the door, his back still against it. His eyes narrowed to slits. He said: "I think not, my dear Morgan. My wife will have something to say about that."

Jimmy held one of Lois's hands tightly in his.

"Something to say—not altogether in your favour, Sanpell. She was taken to Leng Foo's house—half-murdered, herself, and she saw what happened to me. She won't help you, Sanpell. Your day's finished. It's Lois's day now. You've shot your last bolt."

Philip bit his lower lip. But he laughed. His body shook with malicious laughter.

"Have I? You go too fast, Morgan. You may imagine my wife will give evidence against me; though, mark you, in a court of law, a wife may not give evidence against her husband; but even if Lois wanted to tell the police in K.L. what happened to her or to you in Trengtan, I don't think she will do it."

"She will—won't you, Lois?" Jimmy swung round to the girl. "Darling, you've finished with this brute, haven't you? You'll tell people the truth, and let him go to prison for attempted murder. He deserves it. He's behaved abominably to you. The fact that he tried to finish me off doesn't so much matter. But you —I won't allow you to be tortured any longer. You look desperately ill. Have you been ill, Lois?"

"Yes," she whispered. "I have. Very ill. And it's seemed years—long, horrible years—since I saw you in that dreadful bungalow in Trengtan, Jimmy. Oh, Jimmy, how did you get away?"

"Yes, just for a matter of curiosity—how did you get away, Morgan?" asked Philip pleasantly.

Jimmy stared at the other man. It was his private belief that Sanpell was insane. He did not behave like a normal man. His whole behaviour now, was queer. But when Lois repeated the question, he answered it.

"I was taken down the river by two of Leng Foo's fellows and dumped on a lonely spot on the fringe of the jungle and left there. They took it for granted that I would die either from loss of blood from my wound, from starvation or through some wild animal. I lay there for hours, too weak and sick to move. My arm hurt pretty badly and it was bleeding all the time. I certainly thought I was a 'goner' . . ." he broke off, laughing shortly, but his thin, haggard face worked. A shudder passed through his body at the mere re-membrance of those terrible hours on the banks of the river after Leng Foo's boys had left him. Lois laid her cheek against his hand. She was sobbing quietly.

"My poor Jimmy—my poor, poor darling—"

"I lost consciousness," he went on. "It must have been midnight when I came to again. It was a brilliant moonlit night. I saw a Malay woman kneeling beside me. She was not young, but neither was she old and she seemed quite kindly disposed towards me. She spoke Tamil and I answered her in her own language. I told her how I came to be there. She said she could do nothing for me because her husband was in Leng Foo's service. I begged and begged her to help me and she seemed sorry for me.

"At last she promised to do what she could, if, when I managed to escape I would take her with me. She apparently had a very cruel husband, and she hated Leng Foo and his associates. She was one of those very high-minded, noble Malays that one finds out here—a fine character really. Anyhow, she happened to be in that lonely spot on the edge of the jungle that particular night because she had lost a little goat and she was searching for it; afraid she would be beaten by her husband if she did not find it."

"Oh, Jimmy," breathed Lois. "And did she help you?"

"Yes, she gave me a shoulder, and I managed to stumble along with her to a fairly dry and decent part of the country, where she left me on a sort of improvised bed made of twigs and leaves, under the shelter of a mangrove. She bathed my arm and tied it up with strips torn from her petticoats. She was wonderfully kind—I shall never forget it—" he added huskily. "Well, she managed to hide me there for days, until my arm had begun to heal, and she brought me food every night when her husband was out.

125

Through her I managed to live—though God knows I nearly died of fever and exhaustion."

"Jimmy—Jimmy—" Lois was bathing his hand in tears.

"It's all right, darling," he said tenderly. "I'm alive and kicking now."

"So it appears," said Philip malignantly.

"You swine," said Jimmy. "If you had had your way—I'd have rotted on that river bank, wouldn't I?"

"Jimmy, tell me more—how you got back," whispered Lois.

He had little more to tell. Thanks to the devotion of the Malay woman, who had, apparently, taken a fancy to him, Jimmy grew well enough to move, and then, under cover of darkness, he got away from Trengtan, three days afterwards. The Malay woman came with him. After long hours of trekking and picking up what food they could, they reached Kuala Lampor. It had been a long time—many weeks of suffering and danger. But here he was. . . .

"And the woman, God bless her, where is she?" asked Lois.

"Outside the bungalow now," said Jimmy. "She has only one wish, Lois. To serve you. I have told her all about you and she wants to be your amah."

"She shall be," said Lois wiping her eyes. "Oh, Jimmy, I shall love her for saving your life."

"She's a good soul," said Jimmy huskily. "And I've taught her just enough English for a start. You can teach her more."

"This all sounds very much like an idyll—charming," sneered Philip. "But where do I come in?"

126

"You'll be under lock and key shortly, I hope, San-pell," said Jimmy shortly.

Philip laughed aloud.

"Ha! Ha! Damn good," he said.

"Lois," said Jimmy turning to her. "Come darling, out of this blackguard's house."

"I think not," said Philip stepping forward. "Lois won't leave me now—neither will she allow you to accuse me of any attempted murder."

"She shall," said Jimmy fiercely. "I won't let her show you one grain of mercy, Sanpell, after all you've done to her, let alone my little sister—and to me."

"Ask her," said Philip. "Ask her then . . . if she will go with you."

Jimmy's heart gave a queer jerk. He stared down at Lois. She had dropped his hand and hidden her face on the curve of his arm, leaning against the cushions. Her body was shaken with weeping. He said:

"Lois sweetheart—darling—what is it? You will come with me, won't you?"

She did not answer for a moment. She knew what lay in her husband's mind. Cruel, ironic Fate. But things being as they were, she was up against something stronger than herself. She knew she could not, would not, walk out of this bungalow and send the father of her child to gaol.

"Lois," repeated Jimmy. "Look at me."

She looked up at him. Her small face was ravaged with suffering. Her eyes were like the eyes of a trapped helpless creature.

"I—can't go with you, Jimmy," she said in a hoarse little voice. "Philip is right. He's won again."

"But why?" demanded Jimmy fiercely. "Why should you stay with him?"

Her head drooped.

"Because I—I'm going to have a baby, Jimmy," she whispered.

It was as though she struck Jimmy across the face. His eyes grew dazed. He stared at her.

"A baby!—You—my little Lois—Sanpell's child! Oh, how horrible!"

"Yes, it is horrible," she said. "But I'm afraid it's true."

"You are sure?"

"The doctor is sure and—oh, yes—there's no doubt in my mind," she said. "So you see, Jimmy, I can't accuse Philip of all the frightful crimes he has committed. It would reflect so on my—unfortunate child."

Jimmy put a hand over his eyes. He had imagined many things happening to Lois. Never this. The irony of it, the finality, appalled him. It was the one thing he could not fight against. If Lois was to be the mother of a child how could he prevail upon her to disgrace it ere it was born—put the father of it into prison?

"It's too much," said Lois, her voice broken with weeping. "It isn't fair. Oh, Jimmy I can hardly bear it."

He uncovered his eyes and looked down at her. She seemed so fragile, so unfit to bear a child, and she had suffered so much already at Sanpell's hands. It was a ghastly stroke of ill-fortune that this should have happened, he thought. Then he looked up at Philip who had a gleam of triumph in his eyes. He stared at the man's perfect face, and wondered what devil lay behind that mask—why such a man should be allowed to live.

"God forgive you for this, Sanpell," he said. "It's the vilest thing you've done."

Philip dropped his gaze. He had the grace to redden.

"Oh, go to blazes," he muttered. "I'm not going to be dictated to by my wife's lover."

"He isn't that," said Lois, springing to her feet. She faced her husband for a moment, all the fierceness in her roused; rebellion in her eyes; flaming into her white face. "He's my friend—my most faithful friend. God knows I want him to be my lover. If things weren't as they are, I'd walk out of this bungalow with him now. But as I am to bear your child, Philip Sanpell, I shall stay in my place, here. But I shall make stipulations. If I stay—if I keep silent about the things you did in Trengtan, if I ask Jimmy to keep silent too (though heaven knows why he shouldn't take his own revenge), but if he keeps quiet, for my sake—I'm going to have things more my way than yours, in future. Do you understand?"

Philip licked his dry lips. He had never known this new Lois; so strong and resolute, and he ached to defy her. But two things kept him back. One cowardice, the certain knowledge that if Lois and Jimmy chose, they could get him into prison; the other a certain respect for her, the woman who was to bear his child. In Philip's inner-most soul there lurked shame —shame for the thing he knew himself to be.

"Oh, all right," he mumbled. "As you like."

Lois drew a deep breath.

"Very well. I will stay in your bungalow if you will leave me absolutely alone and if you will allow Jimmy to see me, knowing perfectly well that we will keep the law and abide by it, which is more than you have ever done. And if I may have this Malay woman, who saved Jimmy's life, as my amah, and you get rid of Nurse King, whom I cordially dislike. Another stipulation—Gruyler must cease to be my doctor and I shall have Saunders, the English doctor."

Philip shifted from one leg to another. He disliked all these stipulations. But Lois had the whip hand at the moment. He could not quarrel with her. He said:

"All right. Do what you like."

"Then I'll stay," said Lois. The colour left her face now. She looked pinched and white. She sank back on the sofa. "You see, Jimmy," she added, "it's impossible for me to do anything else but stay."

"I see that," said Jimmy. "My poor little Lois,—I see it. And I also see that my hands are tied. For your sake I shall have to concoct some fairy story about the weeks I've been missing."

"If you will be so—generous," said Lois, her tears falling thick and fast. "Although I know Philip does not deserve any generosity from you."

Jimmy closed his eyes.

"For your sake, even that, Lois," he said.

"Thanks, my dear Morgan," drawled Philip, still insolent.

"Oh, get out of this room," said Jimmy, stung to passion. "It will be better for both our sakes, Sanpell, if we see very little of each other these next few months."

"Quite," said Philip. "It will be also better if you see very little of my wife."

"That will be for her to say," said Jimmy brusquely.

"Leave us now for a few minutes, Philip," said Lois in an exhausted voice.

Philip shrugged his shoulders and strolled out of the room. He was in a furiously bad temper. But he had to control it. He knew it. Jimmy and Lois had him in the hollow of their hands at the moment. But only for the moment. Philip was determined that this state of things should not last. One day, in the near future, he, Philip, would be master again. One day he would gain his ambition, to break Lois's spirit. He had not finished with her yet!

CHAPTER V

THE scene that followed between Jimmy and Lois, was brief and tragic. There was so much to be said ... yet so little!

"Fate has taken any idea of revenge or retribution out of my hands," Jimmy said gloomily. "You're right, Lois, I can't touch that fellow now."

"For the—baby's sake," she said and hid her face in her hands.

"Oh, my dear, the cruelty of it," he said. "You poor, poor little thing."

"Don't pity me—I can't bear it," she said. "I've got to go through with it now, Jimmy."

He could not speak, but the tears came into his tired eyes. He laid his cheek against her hair for a moment. Then he said:

"Beloved, if there is ever anything I can do for you —you know you have only to send for me. There will never be anybody on earth for me—but you."

"Nor for me—but you," she whispered. "And you know dear, if it hadn't been for the child, I would go with you now, to the ends of the earth."

"Lois, it's intolerable," he said with sudden anguish.

"My dear, perhaps I won't live, I'm not very strong. Perhaps we shall die together—the poor little child and I. It's going to be *his* child ... but innocent none the less. Maybe it will be better for both of us if it does not live."

"But you—I can't lose you Lois," said Jimmy. "All

these frightful days and nights in the jungle, when I was facing death every moment, it was the thought of you that kept me going. Lois, Lois, you mustn't die, my beloved."

"I won't if I can help it," she said with a faint touching smile. "Cheer up, darling Jimmy. We shall meet sometimes. And I can only say how dreadfully sorry I am that you have been through so much—through my husband. I don't think he is quite sane, Jimmy. We must try to forgive him on that score."

"And you have to stay with him—live under the same roof," groaned Jimmy. "It drives me mad."

"Who knows—the child may be some comfort," she said wearily. "I can't tolerate the thought of it now—but later—" She spread out her thin hands, with a hopeless gesture.

Jimmy seized her hands and covered them with kisses.

"God bless and keep you, little Lois. I'd better go along to Peggy now, I suppose the poor kid's been anxious."

"I don't know. I haven't seen her or anyone. I think Philip has kept everyone from me. I have only had that hateful doctor and Nurse King."

"But you'll alter all that now," said Jimmy grimly. "Swear to me, Lois, that you'll stand no more brutality from Sanpell."

"No more, if I can help it," she said with the ghost of a smile.

He put an arm around her. For a moment she laid her head against his breast and stayed thus clinging to him. Very gently his kisses fell on her hair, her brow, her eyes. No passion now—only great tenderness, love of the highest kind from this man who loved

133

this woman more than life itself. Then he put her from him.

"I'd better go, Lois," he said.

"Yes, to poor Peggy." She hid her face in the cushions because she was blind with bitter tears. "Goodbye for now, darling Jimmy. Thank you for your generosity to—Philip."

"Don't thank me for anything," he said. He gave her one last glance. How he loathed leaving her under this roof! . . . How fiercely he rebelled against her carrying and bearing the burden of Sanpell's child. Then he walked out of the room. On the sunlit veranda he saw Sanpell lounging against a post, smoking. He walked up to him.

"I'm going," he said. "And understand, Sanpell, if you hurt one hair of Lois's head in future I'll make you pay for it; child or no child."

Philip's eyes sparkled wickedly, but he merely inclined his head.

"Oh, very well, Morgan," he said.

Jimmy turned from him and signalled to a tall, graceful Malay woman who was waiting for him in the garden.

"Go to your new mistress," he said. "And take good care of her."

"With my life, Tuan," said the woman, who had the most profound respect and admiration for the white man who had treated her with a gentleness she had never received in her life before.

Jimmy, heavy of heart, walked down the garden to the car which he had picked up in Kuala Lampor on his way from Trengtan; and set out for his own bungalow.

Philip remained leaning against the post of the

veranda. But as Lois's new amah passed him, he eyed her appraisingly. She was a magnificent creature; beautifully built and with a golden skin and liquid brown eyes. She reminded him of Lalla. Very ugly thoughts came into Philip Sanpell's mind. But he let the woman pass.

Monica King came out to him. She was crying.

"Mrs. Sanpell says I'm to pack up and go," she said hysterically. "What's all this about? I thought you were master here."

"Well, I'm not—at the moment," said Philip with a curt laugh. "So if she wants you to clear out, you'll have to clear, and you can tell Gruyler he needn't come any more either."

Monica blew her nose violently and gave him a resentful look.

"So you're going to turn on us now, eh? Well, I still have a tongue," she said spitefully. "I can talk a bit round K.L., you know!"

"Damn!" said Philip under his breath. But he came forward and flung his arm carelessly about the nurse. "Don't lose your hair, Monica," he said amiably. "We can still be pals. I'll see you sometimes."

Immediately she was in his arms; kissing him passionately. He was bored, but forced to respond. Monica's tongue was too dangerous. He dared not let her use it.

In the sitting-room Lois stood weakly by the sofa, and the Malay woman who had saved Jimmy's life faced her respectfully. Lois immediately liked the young Malay woman who had such a noble head and beautiful eyes. This was an amah she could like and trust; not like that horrible old hag they had left in

Trengtan. She felt that this one would be a tower of strength to her. She held out her hand.

"You will serve me, amah," she said. "Stay with me. I know how good you have been to the Tuan Morgan. I am grateful."

The Malay woman suddenly kissed that small white hand.

"Let me stay with you always, Tuanada," she said. "I will never leave you. The Tuan is a good, great white man. And you are great and good, too. He has said so."

Lois smiled through her tears. Here at least was a friend—somebody who knew and loved Jimmy . . . someone, although only a Malay . . . to help her through the next few weary months.

"Help me to my room, amah," she said. "I am very, very tired."

"I will brush your hair and stroke your forehead, Tuanada," said the Malay woman gravely. "I will bring you sleep."

They went upstairs together.

During the next six or seven months, Lois's life was comparatively peaceful.

Monica King left the bungalow. Philip knew where she was, but Lois neither knew nor cared. Dr. Gruyler received a further cheque for his services, and also departed. And now Lois was in the hands of Saunders, the cheery English doctor who attended all the Europeans in Kuala Lampor. And apart from medical attention, she had a most loyal and devoted servant in the amah Jimmy had brought her.

The Malay woman, by this time, adored Lois—was

rarely apart from her. She told Lois many times that she would rather die than go back to her husband in Trengtan who had been brutal and harsh. Her one ambition now was to nurse the Tuanada's little baby.

Jimmy, himself again, back at work, came at intervals to see his beloved. But he did not come often — for both their sakes. It was so hard to meet — to know there was an insurmountable barrier between them. And it hurt Jimmy so profoundly to see Lois looking more frail, more ill every week as the difficult months slipped by. There was no possible doubt now about the child and he was torn with anxiety. He felt that she could never bring Philip's child into the world and live through it.

Philip, himself, was extraordinarily unlike Philip during those months. He kept to the bargain Lois had made. He never worried her; was not often with her, these days. He stayed out a great deal, for which Lois was thankful. And when he was with her, he treated her gently and with a kind of half-shamed respect. She grew to fear and dislike him a little less, but there could never be anything in the nature of affection in her heart for him, now. He had hurt her too deeply for that. But she tried, as the birth of her child approached, to feel more kindly towards him, and to want the poor baby. But that seemed so difficult. She could not want Philip's child.

She had few friends besides Jimmy and Peggy. Peggy was still in Kuala Lampor. She refused to leave her brother. She knew exactly what he was going through, and she was determined to give him her love and care and try to help him. She went often to see Lois. But the rest of the white folk in the district rather avoided Mrs. Philip Sanpell. There was so much talk about the queer happenings of the last few months; Jimmy Morgan's mysterious disappearance had never really been explained and nobody liked or trusted Philip now. People were sorry for Philip's wife, but that was all.

And then, one hot, golden afternoon the following spring, when Jimmy was sitting with his sister on the veranda of his bungalow, talking about the hopes of the estate, which had been doing fairly well this year —Lois's amah suddenly appeared and saluted Jimmy.

"How is the Tuanada, amah?" he asked.

"Tuanada in hospital in Kuala Lampor," said the Malay woman, her brown eyes full of grief and anxiety. "Tuanada has sent for the Tuan."

Jimmy sprang to his feet.

"Oh, God," he said under his breath. "The child—"

"A little girl was born at five o'clock this morning, Tuan," said the amah. "I could not come before, but now Tuanada has sent for you. The baby lives, Tuan, but the Tuanada . . ." the woman's voice broke . . . "she is not expected to live."

For a moment Jimmy could neither move nor speak. He was too deeply stirred by the news the amah had brought him. His head sank between his hands.

He could not credit that Lois was dying— that she was the mother of a little girl—his lovely Lois, who seemed only a child herself, and whose sufferings had been so intolerable.

It was Peggy who roused him by saying:

"Jimmy, darling, you'd better go at once. Jimmy, courage, old boy. The amah may be exaggerating or they may be giving the most pessimistic news of her at the hospital. Don't think the worst."

He looked up at his young sister. The tears were

running down his cheeks and he was unashamed. "I
expect she will die, Peggy," he said in a hollow voice.
"How could she live through it all? But you're right.
I must go — at once."

"Take me with you, dear, I'd like to see Lois, too,"
Peggy said.

The amah looked at them mournfully. She was
heartbroken about her Tuanada whom she had grown
to adore. She did not even care about the little baby
now. Nothing mattered except the Tuanada. But she
had the tranquillity and patience of her race in hours
of trial. The Malay is brave. There were no tears in the
big brown eyes of the amah whom Jimmy had
brought to Lois. Only a great resignation.

It took Jimmy and Peggy half an hour to reach the
hospital in Kuala Lampor, where Lois had given birth
to her child.

Jimmy hoped ardently that Philip would not be
there. He felt that it would be more than he could
stand to face the cad who had broken Lois's heart and
brought her to her death . . . if death, indeed, it was.
But, of course, Philip Sanpell was there, the anxious,
grief-stricken husband to perfection, his handsome
face ravished. He met Jimmy on the steps of the hospital as though they were old friends, as though he
had never tried to kill the other man, or wanted to
hurt Lois.

"Morgan, old chap, thank God you've come. Lois
is calling for you. My poor little wife! She's been
through hell!"

Jimmy gave him one bitter look, then brushed past
him and walked into the hospital. A nurse in spotless
uniform came up to him.

"You are Mr. Morgan?"

"Yes," said Jimmy hoarsely.

"We have been expecting you. Mrs. Sanpell has been very bad since two o'clock this afternoon, and has asked repeatedly for you."

"Take me to her, please," said Jimmy. Then he added, clenching his hands: "Is she—going to die?"

"I hope not," was the non-committal answer.

Jimmy swallowed hard. The next moment he had been shown into a private ward.

"Go and speak to her, but try not to excite her," whispered the nurse. "Doctor thought it might do her good to see you for a moment, as she has called for you."

He tip-toed to the bed. His heart gave a jerk of frightful despair when he saw her thus—her face a desperate little mask of suffering. Such a changed Lois . . . a Lois that surely would not live the night through.

He knelt down beside her and took her hand. It was hot and limp. He bent over her and laid his other hand on her forehead. How damp it was! The fair, silky hair clung closely to it. And now the golden eyes, dark with agony, looked up into his.

"Lois," he whispered. "Oh, my darling, my darling!"

He did not care who heard what he said. He only knew that he worshipped her—would gladly have laid down his life to spare her this—and that all his love and his longing to help her were futile.

"Oh, Lois," he said. "Speak to me."

The faintest colour came into her cheeks, the veriest shadow of a smile curved her lips.

"Jimmy—darling!" she whispered.

He laid his cheek against her hand.

"Are you all right, my darling?" His voice choked. He could hardly speak.

"I'm—all right. But I feel so tired, and the pain has been so—so terrible," she whispered. "It's getting easier now, but I'm tired—tired of everything, Jimmy. I want to die now. I shall be glad to."

"No, no!" he said in sharp agony. "You mustn't die, Lois. You must live. I want you to, darling, my darling."

"But it's all so—useless . . ." her brows contracted. Tears of sheer weakness rolled down her thin cheeks. "We can never be—together."

"We shall be—we must," he said frenziedly. His only thought now was to save her—draw her back from the valley of the shadow into which she seemed to be sinking so gladly. Poor little Lois. She did not want to live, to face life at Philip's side again. But Jimmy felt that if she died it would be the bitter end of all things for him. He could not let her go—could not!

"Darling, darling, don't die!" he said, covering her hand with kisses. "I can't let you go, Lois. For my sake, stay . . . for the baby's sake. . . ."

"Baby . . ." she gave a long, quavering sigh. "Poor little mite, I've seen her . . . my daughter, Jimmy. She's like me, not like him—poor, innocent baby. She is very frail. She won't live, Jimmy."

"Never mind, you must live for me—my beloved!"

"Oh, I don't want to," she said piteously. "I can't bear any more pain."

"You shan't have to, I swear it," said Jimmy fiercely. "Lois, I swear I shall take you away from Sanpell and look after you myself. Whether the child lives or dies, you can both come to me—you must. Lois, live, live, my darling—for me."

He put his arms about her; drew her fair head upon his shoulder..He smoothed the damp forehead, kissed it again and again, murmured over her incoherently, besought her not to die.

Behind the screen a nurse waited, her brows raised, wondering why this should be allowed. It didn't seem to her right and proper when Mrs. Sanpell's own husband—such a handsome, charming man, too, was actually in the building. But Dr. Saunders had forbidden her to interfere.

"This fellow will save Mrs. Sanpell's life. Leave 'em alone," he had said.

He was right. It was Jimmy who pulled Lois back from the very brink of the precipice. By the force of his love for her, the very power of his wish to make her live, he drew her back over the border to safety. He gave out every ounce of his vitality—held her in his arms; besought her to stay with him until he seemed to infuse the will to live into her frail, pain-ridden body. Panting, she lay against him. But her breathing grew easier and the beat of her pulse stronger. And gradually a look of peace passed across her face; her body relaxed. She gave a long sigh.

"Jimmy—darling—I can't leave you."

"No, no, you mustn't. I can't bear it," he said.

Her feeble hand stole up to his cheek. Just for an instant the beautiful, wistful eyes looked into his. Then her lids closed. She whispered:

"I love you so—"

Then she lay still in his arms. Jimmy stared down at her in terror.

"Doctor—Nurse!" he called hoarsely.

142

Saunders came with the nurse in charge. Jimmy laid Lois back on the bed and moved away. For one paralysing moment he thought she was dead. Then he heard Saunders' quiet voice :

"She's sleeping, Morgan. You've done the trick. Now keep that brute Sanpell away from her, and if she gets through to-night we shall have her well and strong again in no time."

Jimmy was shaking; trying desperately to keep his control. He said :

"I'll keep Sanpell away if I have to swing for it. You know a good bit about their story, Saunders. If ever a man deserves lynching, Sanpell does."

"I know," said Saunders grimly. "He's a double-dyed blackguard. But all the nurses in the hospital are falling for him; raving about his profile. It makes me sick."

"It would make them sick if they knew what he's put Lois through," said Jimmy.

"By the way," said Saunders, walking with him to the door. "The child died a few minutes ago."

Jimmy looked at him swiftly.

"The child's dead ?"

"Yes, never had much chance, poor little thing. But I don't fancy the mother will mind very much."

"She never wanted it," said Jimmy. "And she told me she expected it to die. She may weep for it—she's so tender-hearted—and she's its mother. But damn it, Saunders, it couldn't ever have been a joy to her—with his blood in its veins. Now, when she's well again, she'll be more or less free. I look upon its death as a release for her."

Saunders patted him on the back.

"Buck up, Morgan," he said kindly. "Most folk in

K.L. know about you and the little lady, and they're all on your side, I tell you. It's only some of the fool-women who are still raving about Sanpell's good looks. I hope things will come right for you two, I must say."

"Thanks," said Jimmy. "I hope they will, for her sake. She's stood about enough."

Outside on the hospital steps, in the waning light of the setting sun stood Philip Sanpell. He scowled to himself, pulled a cigarette from its case and stood rolling it between his fingers for a moment. Things were not going as he would have liked. Lois seemed a dying woman, and if she died she would be beyond his reach. That unbroken, gallant, pure spirit of hers would remain invincible. That piqued him. He was also furiously annoyed that he had to act a part and let Morgan see Lois. But he had not dared to refuse when he knew Lois's life hung in the balance, and Saunders had told him that unless Jimmy were sent for Lois might die.

He hung about the big, cool, white corridors of the hospital, waiting for Jimmy to emerge from Lois's room. When he did come, looking haggard and exhausted, Peggy was with him, her hand through his arm. She was crying. For a moment Philip's heart gave a jerk. Was Lois dead?

Then Jimmy looked Philip straight in the eyes. He said:

"Lois is going to get better, Sanpell. And I tell you here and now, when she is better she comes to me. She will never return to your bungalow, so you'd better resign yourself to the fact right now."

Philip looked him up and down.

"Indeed!" he sneered. "And who has said so? You —or Lois?"

"We are both agreed on it," said Jimmy grimly.

"I'm afraid I shall not hand my wife over to you quite so calmly," said Philip. "When Lois walks out of this hospital she walks back to where she belongs —to my bungalow."

"You—!" Jimmy broke off. It was only the fact that his young sister was with him that prevented him using a very ugly word at that moment.

Philip laughed shortly.

"You may be very clever, Morgan, but there's the child, and if Lois leaves me, I keep the child."

"That is precisely what I should have expected of you," said Jimmy. "But fortunately for Lois—and the child—there'll be no question of that. The baby is dead."

Philip swore under his breath. It was not that he had any paternal feeling in him or that he regretted the loss of his infant daughter. He was not the sort of man to give a second's thought to the child. But he had hoped to use it as a lever on Lois once she was well. He saw for the moment that he was beaten. He felt so savage that he would have liked to have pulled out a revolver and shot Jimmy. Curse the fellow! Was he always to triumph? Was he to get Lois in the end?

"No," Philip said to himself. "By heaven—no! I'll defeat the pair of you yet."

At the moment he could do nothing. He gave Jimmy and Peggy an ironic bow.

"Thanks for the news," he said. "Goodbye!"

Peggy shivered. She saw the devil behind the perfect mask. It made her feel physically sick.

"Oh, Jimmy, Jimmy," she said, as she walked out of the hospital with her brother, "that man is the devil incarnate. He isn't even decent enough to be sorry his baby died."

"He's mad," said Jimmy shortly. "But I swear I shall protect Lois from him once she leaves this place. She considered it her duty to stick to him as she was going to have a child; but now it's dead she can't go on sacrificing herself to such a reptile."

"Thank God she is going to live," said Peggy.

"Thank God!" echoed Jimmy.

Lois Sanpell did not die.

She recovered slowly but surely after Jimmy's visit to her. The death of the child affected her only slightly. Knowing Philip as she did, she would always have been afraid that his daughter might grow up like him; or at least with some of his terrible traits in her nature. For the baby's own sake Lois was glad it did not live. For her own sake she was natural, maternal enough, to grieve.

And now as she began to pick up strength, her one wish was to avoid seeing her husband alone and having any exhausting scenes with him. So long as she stayed in the hospital that could be managed. Saunders forbade Philip to be left alone with Lois on the grounds that he entirely upset the patient and put back her progress. So a nurse was always put in the ward with them when Philip called. It infuriated him, but he could not do anything in the matter. He dared not make a public fuss. He was forced to speak unnaturally to his wife, to act the tender and devoted husband. And all the time he was aching to jeer at her, snarl at her, hurt her with rough, brutal love-making.

Lois knew what lay in his mind; read it in his eyes. She never saw her husband enter the ward without shuddering; loathing him. But she, for the sake of appearances, had to submit to his visits.

When Jimmy came, always with Peggy, for both their sakes, she knew exquisite happiness and peace. The sight of Jimmy brought her that peace. The gentle pressure of his hands, the tenderness that lay in his eyes, made her heart brim with love for him. Jimmy was the one and only mortal on earth who knew how to bring peace to her aching, bruised heart, who knew how to bring a smile to her lips—those sad lips which would never have smiled again but for the strength, the courage, the support he had given her.

Peggy's visits, too, brought Lois much happiness, for she confided to Lois that she had fallen in love—with a splendid fellow of whom Jimmy approved!

A young medical man in the hospital, a recent addition to the staff, by name Geoffrey Walker, had seen Peggy at the hospital once or twice, and had fallen very speedily in love with her charming young face and curly head. It did not take Peggy very long to respond to him.

By the time Lois was well enough to leave the hospital, Peggy and Dr. Walker were engaged, and it seemed to Lois that little Peggy was going to find her happiness.

Lois was not at all sure of finding hers. There were so many difficulties ahead. She was so afraid of her husband. She knew that his terrible, cruel passion for her was not dead, and that he would never give her up to Jimmy without a struggle which would hurt them all.

Jimmy was determined however, that Lois should not set foot in Sanpell's bungalow again. He and Peggy came in a car to fetch Lois on the morning she left the hospital. The faithful amah had already packed her beloved Tuanada's trunks, and they had been conveyed to Jimmy's estate.

Philip had tried to prevent this; had even sought to win the handsome Malayan woman over to his side by love-making. But he had met his equal in the woman who had saved Jimmy's life and become Lois's devoted amah. She had responded to his attempts to kiss her with the point of a knife. Philip had retired, too careful of his own skin to try any more amorous overtures.

So, on that golden morning of the Malayan spring, Lois was driven home to Jimmy's bungalow. She sat in the car one hand fast locked in Jimmy's, the other in Peggy's warm fingers. Her heart was overflowing. It seemed really like a home-coming this—to the bungalow which was Jimmy's; to devotion and tenderness from him, her friend and lover; and from his sister.

She still felt weak, but she could walk now, and she had gained weight. Indeed there was quite a pretty colour in her cheeks when she stepped out of the car into the sitting-room of the bungalow, and a light in her eyes which Jimmy was glad to see.

She looked round the room, her eyes misty with tears. There were flowers everywhere—all the flowers Jimmy could find in Kuala Lampor, or out of it. The room was a bower of fragrance and beauty.

"Oh, Jimmy, how sweet of you!" she said.

He went up to her and took her hands. Peggy quietly slipped away and shut the door. For the first time for many weeks Jimmy took Lois in his arms and kissed her not as a brother or a friend, but as a lover. Passionately his kisses fell upon her lips and eyes and mouth, until her cheeks were glowing and her eyes like stars.

"Oh, my darling, my darling!" she whispered to him. "I love you so!"

"I adore you, Lois," he said unsteadily. "Sweetheart, I feel it is wrong of me to do this—but I simply must kiss you. I've been so hungry for your lips, beloved."

"You've been so indescribably good to me, dear," she said.

"Sanpell must release you," he said. "You must be my wife, Lois."

She shivered in his arms.

"I'm afraid of Philip. He won't leave me alone or in peace for long, Jimmy."

"I swear I'll shoot him if he comes here!" said Jimmy.

"You can't do that," said Lois. "It would only land you in prison and rob me of your love. But something must be done."

"Don't worry about him now, anyhow, darling. Sit down—rest—be at peace. It is essential."

He lifted her up, wincing at the lightness of her figure. He placed her in a big armchair, kissed her hands and lips again. Then called for the amah to bring refreshments and a fan to keep away the mosquitoes and the heat.

He could not do enough for her. Peggy hung about trying to serve her. The amah would not leave her shadow. Lois thought how adorable they all were to her, how lucky she was to have such devotion. And she tried to do as Jimmy bade her, to forget Philip and his impossible brutality. And she tried to forget the piteous little grave of her dead infant in Kuala Lampor. But it was difficult. Difficult to forget any of the horror, or sorrow, or agony. While Philip was in the district she felt as though evil things waited to spring upon her from all corners.

However, she spent a marvellously peaceful afternoon and evening. After supper, Peggy's fiancé, young Dr. Geoffrey Walker, motored from the hospital to call on the Morgans. He was not strikingly good-looking, but he was a clean-faced, blue-eyed, thoroughly British young man, with an obvious adoration for Peggy. It made Lois happy to see Jimmy's young sister with him. It made Jimmy equally happy.

"Thank the Lord my kid-sister is safely fixed up and will soon be off my hands," he said laughingly to Lois. "Now I can rest in peace about her. She's too young and pretty to be let loose in this God-forsaken country. Walker's a good boy, and he wants to marry Peggy in June. So he shall. I shall write home to the family and tell 'em to cable permission."

Then he added with a wistful look at Lois:

"You must go back to England, soon, dear heart. That's what you need . . . a little Devonshire air to buck you up. You've had enough of this infernal heat. If only you can get free of Sanpell, I shall take you back to England for our honeymoon."

Lois's heart thrilled at the words.

"If only it could be, my darling," she said.

"It must be," said Jimmy, raising her hand to his lips.

Later when everybody had retired and the bungalow was in darkness, Lois lay awake in the spare bedroom which she shared with Peggy. She could not
sleep. She felt well enough and tired enough for sleep,
but her thoughts were full of harrowing memories of
Philip. She had seen him yesterday at the hospital. As
he had bidden her good-bye he had whispered:

"Don't think you can escape me, my dear."

Those words haunted her now. What would Philip
do? What would his next move be? She was ready to
swear that he would not leave her here in peace and
security for long.

Peggy was sound asleep. Lois envied her her healthy
youth. Then she began to think of Jimmy and a tender
smile curved her lips.

Her eyelids closed. She grew drowsy. Finally she
dozed. She awoke with a violent start, bathed in
sweat, to find hands on her—rough merciless hands.
Her eyes opened wide with fright. But before a single
cry could leave her lips she had been gagged—something stuffed into her mouth, a silk handkerchief tied
round it. She kicked and struggled, tried to moan, but
no sound came. She could only stare, affrightedly, her
eyes full of the most ghastly fear, at the face and
figure of her husband. He must have come on to the
veranda and crept in through the open window without making a sound. He was in white—a white linen
suit. It made his figure look all the more ghostly. And
in the shaft of brilliant moonlight that fell through
the parted curtains, she could see his face. It was livid
and terrible . . . lips drawn back from the teeth; the
face of a snarling demon rather than a man; all good
looks wiped from it utterly. It was the face of a man
who was—mad.

Lois gave one frantic struggle; twitched spasmodically in Philip's arms as he lifted her out of the bed; then fainted dead away. She was still too weak to stand a shock of this kind.

Philip whispered against her ear, words to which she was mercifully deaf.

"I've got you again, my dear, and this time you'll never get away alive. One more hour of love with you, your lips to mine, my little wild bird, then we can die . . . together . . . you and I. I shall shoot first you—then myself! Do you hear?"

She did not hear. Her fair head had fallen back on his arm. Her eyelids were closed, her face white.

In the other bed Peggy turned over and muttered something in her sleep. Philip stepped back swiftly. It was that step that saved Lois. For Philip crashed into a wash-stand in the dark. The clatter of china woke Peggy up. She started up, rubbing her eyes, and said:
"What's that?"

Then she saw Philip Sanpell silhouetted against the moonlit window, and Lois in his arms. She gave a piercing scream.

"Jimmy . . . JIMMY!"

Philip turned and staggered through the window. Lois was still in his arms. Peggy's shrill screams aroused Jimmy who was in the adjoining bedroom. He sprang from his bed; wide-awake at once and on the alert. He happened to look out of his window, which was wide open; saw the figure of a man speeding through the garden with something in his arms. Jimmy's first thought was that it was a burglar. He did not stop to get a weapon of any kind. He just rushed on to the veranda and leapt down to the ground, grimly determined to stop the thief and see what he had taken. Peggy saw her brother in his white pyjamas, with bare feet, running across the garden, and thanked God. She threw a dress over her night-gown and followed.

Jimmy neared the figure of the thief who seemed to be somewhat overburdened, and then with a shock, a sense of acute horror, he realised who the man was and what he carried. Sanpell with Lois.

"Stop, Sanpell—stop I say!" Jimmy shouted hoarsely.

He was coming fast on the other man now; and Philip turned his head, face livid, lips snarling. He saw that he would be easily caught.

"Damn you," he said. "You shan't take Lois from me—you shan't!"

He put his wife down on the ground. It was at the bottom of the little tangled garden where a dozen or more rubber trees stood like lean ghosts in the moon-light. Jimmy saw Philip's hand go to his hip-pocket and in a flash he ducked. Just in time. A bullet whizzed over his head. Philip was quite mad; firing recklessly. But he seemed to have no vision. Madness was dis-torting his sight. The shots went wide and the next instant Jimmy had sprung at him; was grappling with him, trying to get the revolver from his hand.

Peggy rushed up; knelt down beside Lois; untied her gag. Consciousness returned to Lois and she opened her eyes to see her husband and her lover locked in that terrible embrace. Her heart seemed to fail her.

"Oh, Peggy, he'll kill Jimmy—he's mad—he'll kill Jimmy!" she wailed.

Then suddenly a shot cracked out. But this time Philip had fired the last one and his hand was in a position so that the bullet went straight through his own head. He crashed down on the ground and lay there motionless. Jimmy stood swaying a moment, breathless, horrified. Then he saw what had happened. Philip Sanpell was dead. He had shot himself. Retribution had overtaken him.

Jimmy did not touch the body, but he knew from the peculiar position of it, from the staring horrible eyes, that Sanpell was no more. He turned to the two girls who were crouching on the ground.

"Peggy, go and 'phone for the police—quickly," he said hoarsely. "Leave Lois to me."

Lois gave one shuddering glance at the body of her husband, then buried her face against Jimmy's arm and the tears came. A torrent of tears, scorching her cheeks.

"Take me home again, Jimmy," she sobbed. "Take me home. . . ."

That ended Philip Sanpell's unspeakable career. And it also ended Lois's tragedy. After that terrible night there were one or two unpleasant moments to be gone through; the inquest on Philip's body; the funeral. But the end meant peace and satisfaction. The verdict brought in by the coroner was "Suicide whilst of unsound mind". Jimmy was entirely exonerated.

There came a time, many months later, when Lois was able to forget the husband whose handsome face had masked such a terrible character; and to forget all the agonies she had endured through her mistaken marriage to him. There came a spring when she was thousands of miles away from Malaya in Devon, on her honeymoon with Jimmy.

And then she was a changed Lois—the sort of Lois Jimmy had known and cared for in his boyhood—a laughing light-hearted Lois with round, pink cheeks and eyes like golden stars. A woman to whom life meant love; and love meant Jimmy, her husband.

Lois never went back to the East. It held such terrible memories for her. Jimmy sold his rubber estate and came home for good. He had other chances in England. Soon after his marriage to Lois he was appointed managing-director of a big motor-tyre company in London. And it was in grey, homely old London-town, two years later, that Lois's son was born, Jimmy's son—with round healthy limbs, his mother's golden eyes and the makings of another Jimmy.

Jimmy knelt by Lois's bedside and was dumb with wonder and amaze at the sheer beauty of Lois with her tiny son in the curve of her arm.

"Oh, Jimmy darling, how happy I am," she said.

"I'm a proud man, Lois, sweetheart," he said.

"Kiss your son," she said.

Jimmy did so in all humility and adoration.

"Kiss me again," said a drowsy, happy Lois.

"Oh, beloved!" he said chokily. "God bless you both."

DENISE ROBINS

CLIMB TO THE STARS

The journey to Morocco should have been exciting and enjoyable for Jane Daunt but it had been turned into a nightmare by the behaviour of those about her.

She had watched the whims of her beautiful cousin Sonia, and seen their effect on the chauffeur, Pat Correl, – and had suffered as a silent spectator to their romance. For Jane herself was deeply in love with Pat, but she could not tell him of her feelings or of her cousin's deceit, and she knew that he would have to suffer, as she did.

CORONET BOOKS

DENISE ROBINS

FORBIDDEN

Two young lovers seeking the atmosphere of peace and tranquillity they were never able to find in London emerge from a car in a sunlit Provençal town square. It was an idyllic setting for a passionately romantic interlude, but the dazzling light and contrasting deep shadows echoed the pattern of their own life, for Nat was a brilliant young surgeon with a professional reputation to uphold and Toni was married to a vindictive business tycoon.

CORONET BOOKS

DENISE ROBINS

BETRAYAL

Nicola was very young and completely bewitched by the well-known novelist, Laurence Gray. He lifted her out of the suburbs into his spoiled luxury world. He led and she followed, despite the protests of her family.

But Nicola had to grow up very fast with Laurence's wife and daughter in the foreground, and worse still, the slow awareness that Laurence was a man of short-lived passions.

"The Queen of Romance still reigns"

Daily Express

"Rarely has any writer of our times delved so deeply into the secret places of a woman's heart"

Taylor Caldwell

CORONET BOOKS

DENISE ROBINS

MOMENT OF LOVE

"You're a romantic little soul – you'll have to be careful or one day you'll be badly hurt" Barbara had warned Christa, and it was true that Christa wanted desperately to be loved – and to fall in love. But when the two friends travel to France for their holiday, they both fall in love with the same man – debonair Stephen Harrimay, a director of one of the largest *parfumiers* in Paris. And the experience has repercussions that affect their whole attitude to life – and to love.

"Few, if any, women writers can equal the remarkable popularity of Denise Robins"

Daily Mirror

CORONET BOOKS

ALSO BY DENISE ROBINS

IN CORONET BOOKS

☐	19479 0	The Other Side of Love	50p
☐	01903 4	Betrayal (*Previously* Were I Thy Bride)	50p
☐	20654 3	Second Best	50p
☐	00745 1	Fever of Love	50p
☐	02474 7	Moment of Love	50p
☐	02922 6	Loving and Giving	50p
☐	02920 X	Lightning Strikes Twice	50p
☐	01437 7	Nightingale's Song	50p
☐	12784 8	Restless Heart	50p
☐	14985 X	The Untrodden Snow	50p
☐	12792 9	Climb to the Stars	50p
☐	02435 6	Slave Woman	50p

*All these books are available at your local bookshop or newsagent, or can
be ordered direct from the publisher. Just tick the titles you want and fill
in the form below.*

Prices and availability subject to change without notice.

CORONET BOOKS, P.O. Box 11, Falmouth, Cornwall.

Please send cheque or postal order, and allow the following for post-
age and packing.

U.K. – One book 18p plus 8p per copy for each additional book
ordered, up to a maximum of 66p.

B.F.P.O. and EIRE – 18p for the first book plus 8p per copy for the next
6 books, thereafter 3p per book.

OTHER OVERSEAS CUSTOMERS – 20p for the first book and 10p
per copy for each additional book.

Name...

Address...

....